MONSTER JUICE

Zits from Python Pit

NO LONGER PROPERTY OF
SEATTLE PUBLIC LIBRARY

D1054003

by M. D. Payne

Grosset & Dunlap
An Imprint of Penguin Group (USA) LLC

To my Gramps, the original crazy old vampire

GROSSET & DUNLAP
Published by the Penguin Group
Penguin Group (USA) LLC, 375 Hudson Street, New York, New York 10014, USA

USA | Canada | UK | Ireland | Australia | New Zealand | India | South Africa | China

penguin.com
A Penguin Random House Company

If you purchased this book without a cover, you should be aware that this book is stolen property.
It was reported as "unsold and destroyed" to the publisher, and neither the author nor the publisher
has received any payment for this "stripped book."

Penguin supports copyright. Copyright fuels creativity, encourages diverse voices, promotes free speech,
and creates a vibrant culture. Thank you for buying an authorized edition of this book and for complying with
copyright laws by not reproducing, scanning, or distributing any part of it in any form without permission. You
are supporting writers and allowing Penguin to continue to publish books for every reader.

The publisher does not have any control over and does not assume any responsibility for author or
third-party websites or their content.

Text copyright © 2015 by M. D. Payne. Illustrations copyright © 2015 by Penguin Group (USA) LLC. All rights
reserved. Published by Grosset & Dunlap, a division of Penguin Young Readers Group, 345 Hudson Street,
New York, New York 10014. GROSSET & DUNLAP is a trademark of Penguin Group (USA) LLC. Printed in the USA.

Cover illustrated by Keith Zoo.

Library of Congress Cataloging-in-Publication Data is available.

ISBN 978-0-448-48247-7   10 9 8 7 6 5 4 3 2 1

Prologue I

Let me tell you about *He Who Would Save Us* . . .

It was said that he would come. But when it happened, it wasn't a man in a huge silver plane as I always thought it would be. No, it was a boy who rode on the backs of crocodiles. It was a boy who saved my poor old friends and brought peace once again to The House of Eternal Rest.

The boy's golden hair was nearly black with mud as he dog-paddled with an unthinkable energy up the White Nile. His journey had started weeks before, deep in the base of a mysterious pyramid, thousands of miles north from where he now swam.

He didn't come alone. Following him along the shore was a tired but determined group of monsters, children, and one adult. All of these people—each one his friend—desperately wanted to stop him, for they didn't realize he had great work to do, a great mission to fulfill.

He Who Would Save Us ignored his friends as they struggled to keep up with him along the riverbank. He gasped and wheezed as he pushed against the current, ignoring their incessant meddling.

"Chris!" yelled the pale man in the suit who led the group on the shore. "You have to stop!"

Behind the pale man in the suit, whom I would come to know as Director Z, the monsters nodded in agreement as they ran. There were seven monsters in all: a waterlogged zombie, a werewolf, a vampire, a Bigfoot, a banshee, a swamp creature, and a small cat-faced lizard creature who I was told came from the moon. Four children, the same age as He Who Would Save Us, struggled to keep up. All of them pleaded for the boy to return to the shore.

"I have to go," the boy yelled between strokes. "I have to go south."

He Who Would Save Us was crazed, his eyes wide open, his mouth crooked but determined. He swam like no human should ever be able to swim, using the strength given to him by his power stone—the same power stone that called him to my people.

As he swam, a crocodile slunk into the water.

Seeing the reptiles, the scaly green swamp creature, who went by the name of Gil, jumped into the churning brown water.

SNAP!

Powerful crocodile jaws nearly crushed the skull of the swamp creature.

Let him go! I wanted to scream, but I couldn't let him or his friends know that I was watching.

"You've been in the water for at least thirty miles," Gil said to our young savior. "Time to get out before you get some kind of weird river rot."

"Gil!" Director Z yelled from the shore. His black suit coat was wrinkled from running, but there wasn't a drop of sweat. "Bring him up here at once. We have to figure out what to do with him. He's gone mad."

"Yes, Boss," said Gil. "I'm happy to get out of here!" He burst out of the water with the boy before the crocodile could charge again.

"Nooooo!" He Who Would Save Us screeched. "Must go south! Now! Let me go!"

The gang of monsters surrounded him at the riverbank and pulled him up the shore.

He Who Would Save Us struggled to push the monsters away. But they were young and strong, unlike the demented residents of The House of Eternal Rest.

"I have to do this," he said, frothing at the mouth

like a hungry hyena. "Let me do this. It's already been long enough."

But they held him down.

The children, out of breath, finally reached the monsters.

"Guys, slow down!" the boy called Shane said. "We can barely keep up."

"Yeah, well, we almost lost him," said the werewolf, who was called Pietro. He Who Would Save Us tried to run again, but the large, woolly Bigfoot named Roy held him down tightly.

"LEEEET ME GOOOOOO!" he yelled.

"Shhhhhh!" scolded Director Z. "You're making the crocodiles hungry."

"That crocodile looked hungry already," said the athletic boy, Gordon. He flexed his biceps and peered out over the river. "Just try that again. We'll be ready!"

"Is Chris cursed?" asked the sickly boy named Ben. "Nabila, can you try a spell?"

"I've never seen anything like this before," said the Egyptian girl with glasses, Nabila. "But I'll try." She took her hands off of her fanny pack and raised them. "ANUBIS-RA-SET!"

But He Who Would Save Us just kept struggling.

Suddenly the water exploded with crocodiles. Teeth flashed as the reptiles pounced on the group, scattering them with fright.

But He Who Would Save Us was not scared.

He jumped onto the back of one of the crocodiles and kicked his heels into the river creature's side.

The crocodile jumped, turned, and crashed back into the water.

SPLASH!

"Wahooooo!" yelled He Who Would Save Us, and the crocodile swam swiftly upriver.

"Catch him, Roy!" Director Z yelled so loudly that the trees shook and squawking birds took flight.

"Sorry, Boss!" the Bigfoot said to Director Z. "All the teeth scared me."

The big monster whimpered and shivered.

"And why didn't you try to speak with them?" Director Z asked Gil.

"I'm a fish, not a reptile," he replied. "And don't you know what crocodiles eat?"

"Bigfeet?" asked Roy.

"No, they eat fish!" yelled the swamp creature. "They eat *me*!"

"Well, we can't just stand here and argue," said Nabila.

"You're right, but we can't keep running, either," said Director Z.

"Well, think of something," said Gordon. "We have to get him so we can get outta here and back home! We've been on the move since taking off from Gallow

Manor, and that was after a week of hard work getting all the old monsters settled after Raven Hill Retirement Home was destroyed."

"At least they're not oldy-moldy anymore," interrupted Shane. "They've been lookin' good since we destroyed Zorflogg on the moon."

"I missed football tryouts while we were on the moon," said Gordon. "I was hoping for hockey, but tryouts were a few days after we escaped from Murrayhotep's pyramid. If we don't hurry, I'm going to miss soccer tryouts, too!"

"Forget about soccer season," said Ben. "If we don't catch up to Chris soon, we're going to lose him. How are we going to catch up to him?"

"Gil, I believe you can help us," said Director Z.

"Well, I should have eaten more leafy greens today," said the swamp creature, "but I'll do my best."

Gil walked knee-deep into the water and then squatted down.

BLLLLLLLLLLLRRRRRRPPPPPPPPP.

The water bubbled violently, popping with green bubbles.

"I see there are a lot of Earth customs I need to learn," said Twenty-Three, the strange combination of cat and lizard from the moon.

A pungent odor filled the air. "I've made the call," said Gil. "It shouldn't be long now."

But the friends of He Who Would Save Us still waited at the riverbank as the sun set.

"We can't wait any longer!" said Nabila.

"Monster transport can take some time," said Director Z.

"Gil was calling for monster transport?" asked Gordon. "That's why he beefed into the river?"

"River transport is usually hiding deep in the darkest recesses of a river," said the swamp creature. "My Emergency Fart Call can reach those darkest recesses, but the speed of sound is only 1.5 kilometers per second in water, and this river is over 6,800 kilometers long."

"It could take more than an hour for the message to reach the transport," said Ben.

"Show-off," said Gordon.

"Nabila's right," said Shane. He paced around nervously. "We might not have much time. I'm really worried about him."

"I'm worried about him, too," said Gordon. "And I'm worried about my face. I'm breaking out like crazy in this heat." He reached up and rubbed the swollen red dot on his forehead. "Grigore, can you pierce this thing with your fangs?"

"Blech!" replied the vampire.

The waterlogged zombie who once surfed the waves of the tropics and was called Clive pointed down the river. "Yo, I think it's finally here," he said.

"Vat is it?" asked Grigore. He giggled with excitement. "Giant flesh-eating vater plants?"

"Ooooooh, a chariot pulled by zombie hippos?" asked the pale and beautiful banshee known as Clarice. The wind blew her hair as she scanned the river.

"No, wait, lemme guess," said Pietro. "Zombie pirate ship!"

"What is that?" Shane asked. He squinted in the fading daylight, trying to make out the large object that was making its way upriver to them. "And what is that terrible smell?"

Prologue II

"It is a ship!" exclaimed Clive.

The ship's sails were full with a great, stinky wind. The odor of rotten eggs strengthened as the huge wooden ship with beautiful, tall white sails approached. The heads of the monsters and children cocked to the side in wonderment. "That's certainly the biggest monster transport I've ever seen," said Director Z.

The others nodded in agreement.

"It looks so nice, I vouldn't even believe it vas monster transport if it veren't for the smell," said Grigore. He waved his hand in front of his nose. "Voo, it's almost as bad as garlic."

"Yet somehow," said Gil, breathing in deeply, "there's something very familiar about that odor."

The bow of the massive ship turned directly to the shore they all stood on. It was coming in swiftly, carried by the stinky winds.

"Um, should we move?" asked Gordon.

"No, monster transport has never harmed a monster or his friends before," said Pietro.

"Yet," added Clive.

Gordon turned to leave.

"It's fine," said Pietro, who held the boy in place.

The ship crashed into the sand of the shallows, but kept moving, creaking and groaning as it made its way to them.

"Ahhhh!" yelled Gordon.

With a great GROOOOOOOOOOOAN, the massive ship stopped an inch in front of the boy's nose and loomed above them.

Gordon turned around. "Well, it might not have harmed me, but it harmed my underwear."

A rope made of leathery boa constrictor carcasses, tied together in skillful knots, fell over the side of the ship.

THUNK.

Pietro tilted his head back and yelled, "Any zombies up there?!"

There was no answer.

Nabila walked up and tugged the rope. The squishy sound of rotten, dead flesh filled the air. "Ugh, this is disgusting."

"At least they're dead," said Ben. "I can't stand snakes."

Everything went silent again as each wondered if another would make the first move.

"Well, let's get going, then," said Shane. He jumped onto the rope and quickly shinnied his way up, pausing at each knot to catch his breath.

SQUISH SQUISH SQUISH.

The Bigfoot quickly followed the boy's lead but was held back by the others.

"Maybe one at a time," said Director Z.

"What?!" asked the Bigfoot. "Do you think I'm fat? You know I've been trying to diet. Meanies!"

"You're a half-ton Bigfoot," said Director Z. "I think it's best that there's not any extra weight on the line when you head up."

They slowly made their way onto the ship in the moonlight.

"Zom-bie piiiii-rates?!" sang Pietro. "Oh, zom-biee piiiiiiiiiii-rates?!"

"Hello?" said Ben. "Is anyone on this ship?"

"Maybe it just takes us where we want to go," said Shane. He walked up to the massive ship's wheel at the front of the bow and put his hand on it. "We're ready to go! Take us to our friend Chris!"

The ship shuddered, and the water underneath it bubbled and frothed. It pulled away from the shore a few yards, the bow swung back out and pointed downriver, and then the ship stopped.

"Why isn't it moving?" asked Nabila.

Dozens of scaly green monsters just like the swamp creature stood on the moonlit shore.

"My African swamp creature brethren!" yelled Gil. "I *knew* I recognized the smell of that ill wind!"

The scaly green creatures were beautiful, their shiny, wet scales gleaming majestically in the moonlight. They waved and threw their hands in the air.

"Gil, are they going to push the ship along?" asked Shane. "Should you jump out and help them?"

The scaly green creatures stopped waving and turned around.

"Hey, guys!" yelled Ben. "What are you doing? We should get going!"

The scaly green creatures bent over with a flourish and . . .

BLUUURRRRTTTTFFFFTTTFFFTT!

. . . pushed the ship into open water by farting in perfect unison.

With a SNAP, the sails were filled with the Stinky Winds, and the ship pushed out into the center of the river.

A green haze drifted down on the passengers, and they began to cough.

The scaly green creatures jumped into the water and followed the ship as it picked up speed and raced upriver at a dizzying pace.

Just as the sun rose, He Who Would Save Us was spotted from the monster transport.

The boy's friends were all crowded around the bow of the ship, pointing and yelling.

"Chris!" yelled Director Z at the top of his lungs. "Stop this instant. Get off of your crocodile and return to the safety of this ship."

The boy savior said something, but the huge GUSSSSSSSSSSSSSH of water drowned out his voice.

He Who Would Save Us and his trusty crocodile were about to be crushed by a massive waterfall.

"Chris!" yelled Nabila.

His power stone, the source of his strength, was also the source of his madness. There was no stopping him—not even a waterfall that could kill him.

"Yah!" He Who Would Save Us yelled. He lashed his crocodile with a reed and held on tightly. "Keep swimming!" The majestic river creature obeyed and swam slowly against the spray of water coming off of the waterfall.

"We have to do something!" yelled Shane.

"He cannot survive this," said Director Z. "But the ship can." He pointed to the largest sail. "That can be opened up even more! Release the rope at the top."

Without a word, Shane took a deep breath and climbed up the mast and into the green haze. For a moment there was nothing but the sound of GUSSSSSSSSSSSSH.

With a SNAP, the Stinky Winds blew the sail open, and the ship lurched forward, heading directly for the boy savior and the waterfall.

"I hope we can gain enough speed," said Director Z. "We must find a way to snag Chris from the water!"

Shane nearly blew off of the mast as the ship hit the rapids at the base of the waterfall.

Gil yelled as loudly as he could above the great din of the quickly moving water. "Help us, my stinky African brothers, or we're going to crash!"

"We're going to hit Chris," said Shane from the mast.

But it was too late.

The ship slammed into the boy . . .

. . . at just the right moment.

As the ship rocked into the froth at the base of the waterfall and began to travel up—yes, up!—the waterfall, the boy savior and his crocodile splashed onto the ship.

"Leave me alone," screamed He Who Would Save Us, shaking with anger, clutching his crocodile tightly.

The ship tilted ninety degrees and headed right up the side of the waterfall into the blue tropical sky.

"Hold on!" yelled Director Z.

"Yeah," yelled Clive, "this is one killer wave!"

The crocodile landed on the swamp creature with a growl.

"No!" Gil screamed. "I'm a bony fish. Bony fish!"

With a screech of fear, the Bigfoot grabbed the crocodile by its tail and flung it off of the ship. Luckily he flung the poor creature far enough that it wasn't crushed by the waterfall. It rose to the surface and watched in surprise as the ship slowly made its way up to the top.

Groans and moans could be heard from the pile of monsters and children as the ship crested the top of the waterfall and splashed horizontal again. They spilled out onto the poop deck.

"Where's Chris?!" yelled Shane.

"Over here!" Twenty-Three yelled.

The best chance for our people's survival lay at the back of the ship, his head smashed through a small wooden door into a cabinet that held rope.

Twenty-Three tried to pry open the door, but couldn't.

The boy savior's arms laid motionless.

"Chris! CHRIS!!!"

WHERE.
AM. I?!

It was dark and moldy, and my head hurt terribly.

"Chris!" someone yelled.

Who is Chris? I thought.

There was a great SNAP of wood, and light filled the hole my head was stuck in. I could see perfectly coiled white rope in front of me. A wet smell drifted to my nostrils.

"His eyes are open," someone said.

"He's stunned but okay!" someone else called out.

"Chris!" a kid yelled. "Are you okay?"

Someone grabbed me and pulled me out of the wooden cabinet my head had been smashed into. The

light shot through my eyes, and my head exploded in pain.

"Uuuuugh!" I moaned.

"Chris, are you okay?" someone asked. I opened my eyes just a little bit and saw a familiar-looking kid. Next to him was a cat-size lizard with fur. I shook my head and it was gone.

"I don't know who this Chris person is," I said. "I haven't seen him. But I think I'm seeing things. My name is . . ." I clutched my head in pain, trying to remember my name. "My name is . . ."

"Your name is Chris," said a pale man. He reached out and clutched my shoulder to hold me steady and calm me.

"Director Z," I said. "I have no idea how I know, but your name is Director Z. And my name is Chris."

The word *Chris* still seemed like something a baby might say while spitting up milk, but I knew it was my name.

My headache went from skull-splitting to merely mind-scrambling, and I took a look around. We were on a pirate ship in the middle of a river. Jungle spilled out into the river on both sides.

"Do you remember me?" asked a dark, curly-haired boy.

"You're a karate master," I said. "Master Shane."

"Yeah!" said Shane, and he clapped my back so hard

my head split open again. "He's back, everybody! Chris is back!"

I looked around to see other friends cheering along with Shane. My friends—Gordon, Ben, and Nabila. I was trying to remember what exactly Director Z was a director of when a low growl shook me from head to toe.

GRRRRRRRRRR.

Mixed in with the cheering, I could hear growls. I looked past my friends, and that's when I could finally see, in the bright, bright sun, a vampire, a werewolf, a zombie, and more monsters staring back at me.

Glaring at me.

"We're on a ship with monsters," I said, panicking. "I *did* see a cat-lizard thingy." My head spun.

"Hi," said the cat-lizard thingy.

I looked around, but there was nowhere to escape. I was, in fact, stranded on a pirate ship with monsters.

The monsters approached me from all sides. Before I knew it, there was a Bigfoot and a banshee in my face.

"So glad you're back," the Bigfoot said.

He reached out a paw, and I flinched.

"What's wrong?" asked Shane.

"Get these monsters away from me," I hissed, and rushed under Shane's sweaty armpit. I was so scared, I didn't even care how bad Shane's BO was. And it was pretty bad. *Why is it so bad?* I thought. *How long have we been out here . . . ?*

"These monsters?" said the vampire. "Vhat do you mean, 'these monsters'?"

"They're talking," I said, huddling deeper into Shane's armpit. "Why are they talking?"

"Darned tootin' we are!" growled a hairy-faced gentleman.

I looked around desperately for something I could defend myself with. But the monsters kept reaching for me.

"Why aren't any of you guys doing anything?!" I yelled.

My friends looked at me like I had a shrunken head.

"What do you mean?" asked Ben. "Are you frightened of these guys? Wow, I guess you really did hit your head hard."

"Ow, don't remind me," I said, and clutched my head.

The vampire reached out and touched my shoulder. "You're okay, Chris," he said.

The way he smiled made me relax. He looked straight into my eyes, and my headache melted away.

"Yes," I said, suddenly filled with love for the monsters. "Yes, I am okay, and I must go—"

"Don't even start that again," said Shane. "Why do you want to go south, anyway?"

"Did I say I wanted to go south?" I said, forgetting where I was for a second.

"Someone or something is compelling you to head south," said Director Z. "We don't know why. But what we do know is that you had us all very scared as we searched for you along the banks of the Nile. We took a day to gather supplies and have been at it for a few weeks now."

"Weeks?!" I said. "I feel like I was just at the pyramid a few hours ago. Back with Murrayhotep."

"Murray," corrected Shane.

"Right, Murray," I said. "He's the last thing I remember before . . ." I stared into the jungle.

"Before what?" Shane asked.

"As I was saying," said Director Z, "we searched for you along the Nile for hundreds of miles. We kept seeing brief glimpses of you ahead, and we'd get close and then lose you again from time to time, but in the end, we caught up to you. And when we finally confronted you, you jumped into the river and fought us with crocodiles. If it weren't for blah, blah, blah-diddy blah . . ."

Director Z kept talking, but I couldn't concentrate. I felt antsy.

"Sorry, guys!" I yelled. "I gotta go!" I had to get away from all of these people and monsters keeping me from my mission. *I just wish I knew what my mission is*, I thought. *What's wrong with me?*

I jumped off of the ship and into the cold, churning water.

"Chris, no!" Director Z yelled. "We can't keep doing this! You must come to your senses!"

The swamp creature jumped in after me, hitting the water with a FLLLLLLLLURT to push himself quickly toward me.

"Stay back, you farting motorboat," I said. "I've got places to go and people to see."

FLLLLLLLRRRP FLIP FLUP!

"I'm coming to get you," the swamp creature said. He disappeared under the water.

I was momentarily stunned, not sure what to do.

"Chris, you're getting drawn back to the waterfall!" yelled Director Z. "Come back to the ship *now*."

The current got stronger. I swam forward as hard as I could, but I was getting dragged back to the very edge of the waterfall. I didn't care about traveling south anymore. I had only one thought on my mind as I felt my body being carried swiftly toward the edge:

I am going to die.

A Terrifying
Journey

I slipped closer to the edge of the waterfall. I turned my head and saw the drop-off only thirty feet away. I could hear the CRASSHHHHHHHHHHH of water spilling over the side. My body shuddered as I thought of what it would feel like to have my bones crushed on the rocks.

"Some . . . body," I gasped, "help . . . me!"

I was fifteen feet away from the edge and moving faster. My arms and legs burned.

"Can . . . any . . . crocodiles . . . help?" I said, though I doubted any crocs could actually hear me.

I was ten feet away from the edge and moving

terrifyingly fast. I turned toward the drop-off and tried to figure out how to position my body for the most comfortable death possible.

"Chris," yelled Shane, "don't stop fighting!"

I turned back and swam as hard as I could, but it only slowed me down a little.

"FIIIIIIIGHT!" my friends yelled.

"They're almost there," said Shane.

Who's almost there? I thought.

I could feel myself slipping over the edge, and just as I began to fall . . .

BLLLLLLLLLLLUUUUUURFT!

A great stinky wind blew me off the edge of the waterfall and up into the air.

I corkscrewed through the air, and as I turned, I saw the same group of African swamp creatures that had saved me once before. Now they were flying out from the waterfall, farts blowing majestically upward as they tumbled down to the rocks below.

I landed with a SPLASH and sank deep into the water. I had survived the waterfall thanks to the swamp creatures, but I was too weak to swim. I drifted helplessly, scraping against the muck at the bottom of the river.

Webbed hands slapped my face, and I opened my eyes to see Gil in front of me in the murky water.

Bubbles escaped from his scaly backside. "I told you

I was coming to get you," he fartspoke. He grabbed me and used his powerful webbed feet to push us up to the surface of the river.

"You'll be okay," said Gil. "I've got you now!"

He towed me to the riverbank and laid me on the hot sand.

I lay and breathed in the air. I finally started to feel better. So good, in fact, that . . .

"I'm ready to go, Gil," I said. "Thanks for your help!"

"Oh, no you don't!" said Gil, and he lifted his scaly arm to reveal a hairy, dirty armpit.

"That's disgusting," I said. "I'm getting out of here." I stood up, but was immediately dizzy from the stench of the swamp creature's slimy pit. Gil grabbed me with his other hand and stared into his armpit intently.

"You were almost just killed for the third time in ten minutes," said Gil. He steadied me and then dug around in the hair of his armpit, searching for something. "We can help you get to wherever you need to go, but you need to be sane while you do it. AHA!"

With a slight wince, he pulled out a small brown something. It looked like a raisin.

"Eat this," he said.

"No WAY," I said. "What is it?"

"It's a—"

But Gil was cut off by Director Z. "Back up!" he yelled from the water.

We both looked up to see the pirate ship sailing directly toward the beach we were standing on.

"It's going to crash," yelled Director Z. "The African swamp creatures lost control when they focused all their flatulent energies on you!"

"I don't think it's going to stop this time," said Gil. He grabbed me and jumped up into the jungle above the riverbank.

The ship hit the sand and kept going.

SSSCCCCCCRRRRASH.

Gil and I stuck our heads out of the jungle vegetation and saw the front of the ship twist in the sand and get pulled back out into the current.

"Everyone out!" yelled Director Z. "The current is going to pull the ship to the waterfall."

Roy threw a huge, thick boa-constrictor rope over the side of the ship as it slid away from the shore. The monsters that were able jumped over the edge with a SPLASHSPLAT, and everyone else quickly shinnied down the snake rope.

"Hurry, hurry!" yelled Gordon, who was practically pushing Ben down the rope. "Just jump, it's probably deep enough now."

"Fine, I'll jump if you help me swim to shore," he said.

SPLASH SPLASH SPLASH.

Everyone was on the shore or in the water helping

one another keep from getting sucked into the current as the ship was swiftly pulled away.

"Are the swamp creatures okay?" Nabila asked Director Z as he pulled her up onto the shore. "Is there something we can do?"

"They're probably just stunned by the current under the waterfall," said Director Z. "They'll be fine, but I'm afraid they won't come around quickly enough to save the ship."

"But they did save Chris," said Shane.

"Yes, they did, indeed," said Director Z.

The great pirate ship, its sails completely slack with a lack of stinky winds, tipped over the waterfall with a great CREEEEEEEEAK.

There was silence and then . . .

BOOOOOOOOOOOOOOOOM!

"So much for our monster transport," said Gordon.

"That's all right," I said. "I need to go into the jungle now, anyway, I think. Thanks for all the help, guys."

I turned to leave and was immediately grabbed by Roy.

He flipped me, and Gil once again held up the gross brown armpit raisin that he had tried to feed me before.

I smacked it out of his hand before he could get it to my mouth. It tumbled into the dirt.

A small monkey darted out of the jungle and picked up Gil's sick little treat.

"Give it back!" yelled Gil.

But the monkey ran right past him and scurried up my legs.

"Hey!" I yelled, but Roy held on tightly.

The monkey shoved its hairy black little hand right into my mouth, depositing the putrid armpit raisin into the back of my throat. I swallowed and gagged almost immediately. My throat tasted like the moldiest mushroom pizza in the world.

HWARRRRF.

I dry-heaved so hard that I flung the monkey down onto the sand. It ran back into the forest.

"For the love of Neptune, keep it down!" yelled Gil. "It took years to make."

Tears welled up in my eyes, and my stomach cramped terribly. I squatted on the ground and clutched my knees.

Shane walked up to me and patted my back. "How do you feel?" he asked.

"I feel like I want to throw up through my eyeballs," I said. "And I still feel like I have somewhere to go. But I don't need to rush there anymore."

Shane sat me up on a nearby rock.

"Welcome back, dude!" yelled Clive, and he slapped my shoulder so hard, I fell off the rock.

"Sorry, I got a little too stoked," said Clive.

I passed out in the sand.

Jungle Zit

I woke up in the shade, but I was still sweating through my clothes.

"It's so hot," I moaned. "I feel terrible."

Above me, beautiful tall trees rustled with birds and monkeys that jumped from branch to branch.

Shane walked over and helped me off the ground. Large wet leaves were stuck to my back. "Yeah, Director Z said that you'd be affected by the heat a lot more now that you're not as driven to go south. You were running on pure adrenaline!"

"Where are we?" I asked.

"First of all," Shane said, "*who* are we?"

"You're Shane," I said. "I'm Chris."

"Awesome!" he said. "I just wanted to make sure we hadn't lost you again."

"So, where are we?" I asked again. I looked around to see I was in a rain forest with massive trees. Huge trunks shot up from the ground into the air and were crisscrossed with vines.

Nabila, Ben, and Gordon walked over to me. Nabila held Ben's hand.

"For the record, these two are still boyfriend and girlfriend," said Gordon. "BLECH."

A few trees over, in front of the biggest tree trunk I had ever seen in my life, the monsters stood in a circle with Director Z, quietly reviewing the supplies from Roy's massive messenger bag and planning out our next move. Director Z saw that I had stood up, and walked toward me with a smile.

"We're not sure where we are," said Nabila. "Director Z's not sure. Before you passed out, you told Gil you wanted to go into the jungle. So we headed in."

"How long ago was that?" I asked.

"Two days," said Gordon.

"How do you know we're going in the right direction?" I asked.

Director Z stepped up to us. "Since then," he said, "you've woken up in a feverish panic a few times and pointed in the same direction. You probably don't even remember doing it. But we're assuming that, even with Gil's possession remedy, you know where we should be headed."

"Ugh," I said. My mouth got dry at the thought of the moldy mushroom taste of Gil's armpit raisin. "I had almost forgotten that happened. I wonder where that nasty little monkey is."

"I think he's been following us," said Shane.

Ben raised his eyebrow at Shane.

"I'm pretty sure my barfing scared him off," I said. "That thing tasted so terrible. What was it, anyway?"

"That was a rare fungus that can only be grown in the darkest reaches of the deepest, dankest, moistest cave," replied Director Z.

"That sort of sounds like Gil's armpit," I said. "You just forgot 'hairiest.' So what did it do to me? Is that why I slept so long?"

"No, no, you slept so long because you were finally unhooked from the power that was compelling you to flee south and deep into the jungles of Africa," said Director Z. "The remedy reduced the intensity of the call you are receiving by adding a protective slime layer between your brain and your skull. It's a very effective treatment for migraines as well. Now you can talk with us like a normal human being, and we can all figure out together where it is you need to go and why this is happening to you. I, for one, would like to know what . . .

or who is calling you so urgently."

I looked past the monsters standing in a circle a few trees over and thought, *It's that way.*

"It's that way," I said, pointing confidently.

"What makes you think it's that way?" asked Shane.

"What is the 'it' in question?" asked Director Z.

"I'm not sure," I said. "I just know it's that way."

"Well, that's certainly consistent with the direction we've been headed in so far," said Director Z.

"We can't just keep going because Chris *thinks* he needs to go in a certain direction," said Gordon. "What if that armpit raisin scrambled his brain? I need more details. It's hot. I'm starved. My face is breaking out all over. Look at this zit!" He pointed above his nose. Between his eyes was the biggest zit I had ever seen on anyone from Rio Vista Middle School. "It's so big, I can look at it cross-eyed. So how long will it be before we get to wherever it is we're going, and do they have showers?"

"I feel like it's close," I said, but I had no idea why.

"What about the showers?" asked Nabila. "I could really use one."

I thought long and hard about it, but my brain came up empty.

"I don't know," I said. "I just know that we need to keep going. I've got something really important to take care of."

HISSSSSSSSSSNO!

A snake fell out of the branches above Gordon.

In a flash, Director Z took off his suit coat and whipped the snake before it crashed into Gordon's head. It quickly slithered away.

"AHHHHH!" yelled Gordon.

"Did it bite you?" I asked.

"Are you okay?" asked Director Z.

"Did that snake just say 'no'?" asked Shane.

"My zit," gasped Gordon. "Now my zit feels like it's going to explode."

"So why don't you just pop it?" Ben asked Gordon.

"I need a mirror or something," replied Gordon. "I don't even know how to attack it without one. So why don't *you* pop it for me?"

"Gross," said Nabila. "Just gross."

"Yeah, no thanks," said Ben.

"Director Z," said Gordon, "do you still have that magic telephone that called us on the moon?"

"Yes," said Director Z. "But if you're thinking about calling Gallow Manor, think again. The rest of the monsters are just fine where they are. I can't risk having them take part in what could turn out to be a wild-goose chase."

"Hey!" I said. "This isn't a wild-goose chase!"

"It doesn't matter. I don't want to use it to call anyone," said Gordon. "But a phone that's smart enough to make a call on the moon must also have a camera, right?"

"Yes, it does," said Director Z.

"Can you give it to me?" asked Gordon.

"Do you really think taking a selfie right now is the best idea?" asked Ben.

Director Z handed Gordon the cell phone.

"I'm not taking a selfie," said Gordon. "I'm taking care of business."

Gordon lifted up the phone in front of his face.

"Oh man, you're worse than I thought," he said to the zit. "You've gotta GO."

He brought his thumb and index finger up to the zit, and before Director Z could say *What are you doing?*, Gordon did it.

SPLOPP!

Gordon popped the zit with a satisfied grunt and wiped the pus off of the telephone with his shirt.

"Sorry," he said as he handed the phone back to Director Z. "I wasn't aiming for it or anything."

"Thanks," said Director Z, and he slowly put the phone away in his pocket.

AAAAAAAAAAAAAH!

Over by the tree, Roy started to scream.

The other monsters backed away from him as he flailed and jumped around, crazed.

We ran over to see what was happening.

Deep in
the Jungle

"What is it?!" Gordon yelled, running ahead.

The Bigfoot took a powerful swipe at the invisible enemy. His long flailing arms almost took Gordon's head off. Then Roy stopped swinging. His little-girl screech echoed through the jungle.

EEEEEEEEEEE!

The monkeys popped their heads through the canopy to see what was happening.

Roy dug deep into the fur on his chest, struggling to remove something black that was stuck in it.

"Big spider!" yelled Roy. "Big spider!"

He pulled a fist-size spider out of his fur and threw it on the ground.

He stomped and screeched and stomped some more, shaking the ground everywhere around him. When he was done, he ran around to the other side of the tree to hide.

Grigore walked over to what was left of the spider. "Does anyvone vant a spider pancake?"

"Sort of makes me miss Griselda," said Shane. "She'd love a spider pancake."

"Sort of makes me miss food," said Gordon. "Now we don't have a river filled with fish to eat. And we've run out of flatbread."

"I'm sure we'll be able to find something edible when we get to where we're going," I said. "I can—"

"Feel it," Ben finished. "Yeah, we know. Please tell me you're feeling a McDonald's."

I concentrated really hard, but I couldn't feel it.

"Sorry," I said.

"A good falafel?" asked Nabila.

"Nope," I said.

"Brains?" Clive asked.

"Hmmm," I said.

"Never mind," Clive said. He began to sniff the air. "Smells like a gnarly snack might be nearby."

SSSSSSSSSSSSSSSSNIFFFF!

Clive sniffed so hard that his nostrils flapped.

"Which way are we going?" he asked.

"That way," I said, and pointed.

"Awesome! I think that's where it's coming from," said Clive. "Let's roll!"

Clive took off before I could ask him what he smelled. We all followed.

"Come along, Roy," said Director Z.

Roy shook his head and pouted like an angry toddler. "I'm going back to the river," he said.

"Is that a tarantula coming down the tree?" asked Nabila.

Roy bolted toward us. "Wait for me!" he said.

"Well done," Director Z whispered to Nabila.

Hours later we were still pushing our way through the thick jungle. The monsters were strong and had no problem with the heat. My friends and I were covered in sweat and looked more like zombies than Clive did.

"How's that zit?" Shane asked Gordon.

"It feels a lot better now that I popped it," Gordon replied. "But it still throbs. I feel like someone kicked me in the face."

"Dude, could you please wipe the pus off of your T-shirt?" moaned Ben. "There's so much that leaves are sticking to it."

"Ew," said Nabila.

Gordon stopped to pluck off the three or four leaves

that were stuck to his shirt.

He pulled the first one off, and a tiny snake slipped off the back and onto the ground.

"Gross," said Ben. "Your pus is attracting baby snakes."

Gordon looked down with disgust. He stomped the little snake.

"All right," I said. "Let's go."

"Are we at least close to wherever it is we need to go?" Nabila asked me.

"I have no idea where we are," I said. "But I know we're going the right way."

"Right on, because we're super-close to that gnarly snack," said Clive. He shook with excitement.

"When are you going to tell us more about this snack?" asked Ben.

"Smell for yourself," said Clive.

Ben took in a deep, nasally breath.

"Wh-URP," he said, almost throwing up. "What is that? It smells like rotten chicken."

The rest of us sniffed deeply.

"Ugh," said Shane. "It smells like you, Clive. A rotten body."

"You've got that right!" said Clive excitedly.

"Hey," I called to Pietro. "Can you smell that?"

"Yeah, I've been trying to ignore it for hours," he said. His nose was dripping green goo.

"All right, everyone," said Director Z, pulling out his cell phone. "We should stop soon. The sun will be setting in fifteen minutes or so, and we have to—"

BEEP BEEP BEEP.

Director Z's cell phone tried to jump out of his hand.

"What in blazes . . . ?" he said.

"I don't care about no sunset," said Clive, and he rushed into the jungle toward the rotten smell.

"We can't get separated," Director Z yelled. He looked down at his phone again with a strange look on his face. "Clive, you need to get back here! We've got to set up our protective perimeter. You could be devoured by jungle cats!"

"Should we go after him?" I asked.

Director Z looked at his phone one more time, shoved it into his pocket, and said, "Everybody get him!"

We rushed in the direction he had run.

"Clive!" yelled Shane. "CLIVE!!!"

The monsters tore through the jungle. The farther we pushed, the more terrible it smelled.

"Ugh, what *is* that?" said Gordon.

We crashed into a small clearing and were face-to-face with the biggest, ugliest flower I'd ever seen in my life. It was eight feet tall, with a huge fleshy white structure that shot up from its wrinkly red center.

"It's a corpse flower," said Ben. He turned a little green.

"A corpse flower?" asked Gordon. "Like, a real corpse?"

"No, it just smells like one," said Ben, gagging a little. HWUUUURP.

"Are you kidding me?" said Clive. "It smells like a rose! A rose so sweet I could eat it."

"Ugh, I can taste it in my mouth," said Shane, "and it's not anything close to delicious. I think I need a breath mint."

Clive didn't care. He jumped into the center of the flower and took a big bite out of the fleshy white center. A swarm of startled flies took to the air, buzzing around us.

"It smells like a corpse to attract flies, which pollinate it," said Ben, turning even greener.

I coughed at the insane smell and inhaled a few of the flies.

"Well, at least I'm not as hungry anymore," I said.

"I'm going to—" said Ben.

"We know," the rest of us said.

BAAAAAAAAAAAARF.

"Well, we need to set up camp before it gets too dark," said Director Z. "It will be quicker if you all help Clive clear out the corpse flower. Get to work, everyone. Let's eat all of it. Quickly, quickly!"

"I don't see you jumping in there, Director Z," said Pietro. "This is all Clive." He grabbed a few leaves, rolled them up, and plugged his nose with them. "And I'm not sleeping in his tent. Oh no!"

GROLF GWURPLE SMACK CRUNCH.

Clive chowed down on the flower.

"That's disgusting," said Nabila.

"Well, at least I can finally smell my sweat again instead of a corpse," I said.

I smacked a mosquito on the back of my neck.

"Looks like someone else can smell you," said Gordon.

"Stupid bloodsucker," I mumbled.

"Vhat did you say?" asked Grigore.

"You know what I mean," I said.

More bugs buzzed around our heads as the air cleared and the sun set.

"All right, let's get the tents up and then create a protective line around this area," said Director Z. He turned to Twenty-Three and handed him a bag of black powder. "I think a twenty-foot circle should do just fine."

Twenty-Three ran off into the jungle and started to lay down the line.

"What is that stuff?" I asked Shane.

"We've been using it at night to protect—"

"Help!" yelled Twenty-Three.

I looked toward the scream, and he was gone. The bush behind where he had stood shook and squealed.

"The jungle ate him!" screamed Clarice.

You're Such
a Boar!

"Twenty-Three!" yelled Roy, and he pounded toward the bush that had swallowed the small moon creature.

Twenty-Three popped out of the bush and screamed, "Roy, help!" Roy reached out his paw to grab him, but the bush pulled Twenty-Three back in.

SQUUUUUUUUUUUUUEEEEEEE!

"Is that a splurtsar?" asked Shane.

Twenty-Three burst out of the bush, followed by a small wild boar. "There's something wrong with it. It's crazy or something."

I ran up to the small boar and tried to scare it away.

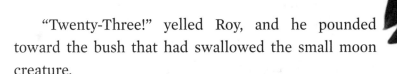

"Be careful!" yelled Nabila.

It jumped and opened up a mouth filled with sharp teeth. Its red eyes stared deeply into mine as it flew directly for my neck.

A screech filled the air as a small monkey crashed into the boar from above. Both slammed to the ground.

Everyone ran over.

"It's a vampire boar!" I told them. "The monkey who made me eat Gil's nasty raisin thingy saved me."

"So that's twice now," said Shane. "Hmmmm . . ."

The monkey darted back and forth to escape the snapping jaws of the very hungry vampire boar.

CRACK!

Roy knocked the boar in the head before it reached the monkey's throat.

"Did it bite you?" Shane asked Twenty-Three.

"My lizard skin kept me safe," he said.

I crouched down on the ground near the monkey. "Are you okay, little guy?" I asked.

The monkey chattered happily and jumped up onto my knee.

"Whoa," I said. "Please tell me you don't have another nasty armpit raisin for me."

SQUUUUUEEEEEEEE SQUUUUUUUEEEEEEE SQUUUEEEEEEEEEE.

I looked down at the boar. It was still passed out.

"Where is that coming from?" Ben asked.

"Everywhere," said Pietro. He quickly turned into a werewolf and raised his hackles.

The monkey jumped to my shoulder and chattered. I stood up quickly.

The bush in front of Director Z exploded with fur and tusks. Three vampire boars jumped out at him. Pietro knocked them out of the way.

"Those guys are huge!" yelled Gordon.

"The other one must have been a baby," said Ben.

Within seconds, a dozen very large, very angry, very hungry boars surrounded us.

They closed in, pushing us all together in a tight clump.

SQUUUUUEEEEE!

One lunged at Grigore, who bared his fangs. "I'm vone of you," he growled.

The boar gave him a strange look and headed on past the vampire.

Gordon rolled on the ground to avoid two boars that came at him from two different directions. They knocked their sharp tusks together and stumbled away.

"Hi-ya!" yelled Shane with a chop to one boar's head. Roy tossed another into the air and, with perfect timing, Shane gave it a powerful roundhouse kick that sent it back into the jungle.

The monkey, still perched on my shoulder, gave a warning screech as each boar charged me, quickly enough that I could dodge them all.

"We're actually going to make it!" yelled Ben. His back was to Nabila, and they helped each other dodge any boars that charged their way.

SQUUUUUUEEEEE! SQUUUUUUEEEEEEE!

Two dozen more boars surrounded us.

The ones we had already managed to knock out woke back up.

"Yaaaaaah!" screeched Clarice. A boar had chomped down on her leg. She yanked it off and threw it into the nearest bush.

"Oh no!" yelled Ben. "Is she going to become a vampire?"

"No, each resident of our retirement home is protected from one another's monstrous powers," said Director Z. He pulled out the Taser he always kept in his suit pocket and zapped another boar. "She'd already be a werewolf if not. She was bitten by Pietro, remember?"

"That protection doesn't spread to us, does it?" asked Shane. He karate-chopped another boar perfectly in the forehead.

"Unfortunately, no," said Director Z.

The boar Shane had just karate-chopped jumped up again.

"How are we going to kill all of them?" shouted Gordon, knocking another boar out of Nabila and Ben's way.

"We don't need to kill them," yelled Director Z. "We just need to incapacitate them."

I kicked another boar in the side of the face, away from his sharp tusk. But we were starting to lose the battle.

"Any ideas?" I asked, panicked.

"Cover me," said Director Z. He moved as far away from the battle as he could and raised his hands. "Boa, Boa, quite constricted, help the monsters most afflicted!"

The jungle rumbled once again, but this time with the sound of . . .

SLITHER SLITHER. HISS.

The boars, despite being so close to mealtime, suddenly stopped and SQUUUUUUUEEEEED in fear.

Massive snakes appeared from every corner of the jungle.

"It's raining snakes," yelled Nabila. One landed right at her feet. She almost knocked Ben over trying to get out of its way.

"They will not harm you," said Director Z.

The boas slithered directly toward the boars. Half of the little piggies were quickly grasped and squeezed, unable to SQUEE. The others scattered and ran into the jungle. The boas followed.

"See, dude, I told you Directors always have something up their sleeves," said Clive.

"Can I learn how to do that?" I asked.

Great Balls
of Something

The protective ring had finally been laid, and the largest vampire boar was roasting over a fire.

"Normally," said Director Z, "I would recommend against this, but considering our situation, I felt it was warranted."

"Recommend against what?" asked Ben. "Eating vampire flesh? Are we going to get terrible indigestion and turn into vampires?"

"No, the meat will not harm you," said Director Z.

"I'm not so sure about that," Ben said. "You know I have a sensitive stomach, right?"

"There are other things to eat in the jungle if you're

not hungry for this," said Director Z.

"Like what?" said Ben, cheering up a little.

"Pietro, can you sniff out a little snack for Ben?" asked Director Z.

Pietro stood up, turned into a wolf, and sniffed the behinds of a few other monsters. He stopped at Gil's backside.

SNIFF SNIFF SNIFFFFFF.

"Hey, I know I have a gas problem, but you don't have to rub it in," said Gil.

Gil stood up and walked away. Pietro began to claw at the log he and Twenty-Three were sitting on. He changed back into human form, pulled up the bark, and drooled a little at what he found underneath.

"Ooooh, eat up, Ben!" said Pietro.

"What?" asked Ben, and he went over to have a better look.

I went over with him and found myself face-to-face with the biggest maggots I'd ever seen in my life. They wiggled and squirmed, upset to be in the open air.

"So juicy," said Pietro. He plucked one out of the wood. "Not one bit of crunch. Perfectly mushy and delicious, just like a small pouch of whipped cream."

Pietro popped the maggot into his mouth, let it squirm around for a moment, and then, SLURRP! "Mmmmmm, that was good."

"I think I'll stick to the hampire," said Ben.

"That's the spirit!" said Director Z.

Once the boar was ready, even a few of the monsters had a bite.

"I'm just really interested in vhat it tastes like," said Grigore as he took a huge bite.

"It tastes really good," I said. I fed a little bit to the monkey, who was still on my shoulder. "I'm amazed I'm not starved, though. I don't remember eating anything while I was on the run."

"Oh, you ate plenty while you were 'on the run,'" said Gordon.

"What do you mean?" I asked.

"You ate anything that wouldn't eat you in the Nile," said Gordon. "You'd take one bite out of a fish and just toss it, which is how we were able to eat so well when we followed you."

"And?" I asked. "Did I eat any of those maggots?"

"Maybe," replied Gordon. "We can't be sure. You weren't always in our sight."

"So what did you see me eat?" I asked, not sure I wanted to know.

Gordon looked like he wasn't sure he wanted to tell. "You feasted for a little bit on a water buffalo that had been dead for a pretty long time. Fur and all. Just a few bites, though. And then there were the fish and cranes and that hippo."

"Hippo?"

"Yes, just one bite," said Director Z. "You crept up from behind and bit its posterior. It was so insulted that it poo—"

"Don't ruin my dinner!" said Clarice. She chewed on a bit of boar tenderloin. "Clive, dear, are you sure you don't want any?"

He answered Clarice by lifting a leg.

FLLLLLLURT.

"Wowee," said Gil, waving his hand in front of his face. "Even I, the Fart Master, must tip my hat to raw power and skill when I see it!"

"What did I say about ruining my dinner?" said Clarice.

"Director Z, Clive can't sleep in my tent," said Roy. "He's going to burn off all of my fur with his mega-farts."

"After what we've just encountered," said Director Z, "it's important for everyone to have a buddy, including Clive, and everyone needs to stay in their tents. Better to be safe and covered in a fart cloud than dead, I say."

"Then why don't you make Clive *your* buddy?" asked Roy.

"Because I'm the Director," he said. "A Director cannot be distracted by a fart cloud. A Bigfoot can. I need to concentrate. There's something else going on in the jungle, something even more worrisome than big cats."

"I've been thinking about the corpse flower," said

Ben. "Those are only found in Sumatra, in Indonesia. Not Africa."

"Correct," said Director Z with a smirk. "Your intelligence is always surprising me in new ways."

"Me too," said Nabila, impressed with her boyfriend. Ben blushed.

"How do you know stuff like that?" Gordon asked Ben.

"How do you know how to kick a field goal?" asked Ben. "You practice at sports. I practice at being a nerd."

"So someone brought a corpse flower deep into the African jungle," said Shane. "Why?"

"I'm not sure," said Director Z. "But its appearance, coupled with the vampire boars, makes me feel like we've stumbled upon some source of monster power. I wonder if all of this monstrous influence is what's attracting Chris."

"But I don't feel like we're where we need to be yet," I said. "Close, yes, but not quite there. I wasn't looking for a corpse flower."

"There's something else," said Director Z. "For an instant, just a few seconds, my phone gave off a very interesting warning alarm. It seems that it may have picked up a distress signal."

"A distress signal?" I asked. "What do you mean?"

"Each retirement home can send a distress signal if the need should arise," replied Director Z. "But I'm not sure if it's real. I don't know of any retirement home in this area. And it was such a brief signal. It might just be that my phone is acting strangely because of our recent trip to the moon."

"Or a retirement home might be in distress," I said. "Am I being called by a retirement home?"

Director Z didn't answer. He sat still in front of the fire. "We'll move on in the morning," he said. "But we should proceed with caution."

"Just to be clear," I said to the monkey, "Shane is my tent buddy. You've gotta sleep outside."

In the morning, we packed up all of our supplies in Roy's huge bag and started walking toward "it" again. It was another sticky day in the jungle. Huge mosquitoes hovered around our faces.

"Good morning, dear friends," said Grigore.

"If one of your dear friends bites me," I said, "I will slap it."

Grigore waved his hand with a flourish, and the mosquitoes flew away.

"You don't have any idea how long until we get there?" Shane asked me.

"No, but I've been feeling calmer and calmer as we move toward whatever it is, and I don't think it's because of Gil's armpit raisin," I said. "I woke up feeling great, so maybe we'll find what I'm looking for today."

"Where's your monkey friend?" asked Shane.

"I don't know," I said. "Maybe he got mad at me after I booted him out of our tent last night."

The sun was high in the sky as we walked through the jungle. We were just about to stop for a break, when Pietro growled.

"There's something nearby," he said, and turned into a werewolf.

"What do you mean?" I asked the angry werewolf. "You can't just turn into a wolf without explanation. Is it big? Is it a monster?"

I looked at Director Z, and he shrugged.

WHOOOOOOSH!

Without warning, a huge white object burst out of a nearby bush and hit Gordon right between his eyes.

"Aaaaargh!" Gordon yelled. "It's killing me!"

Where Are
You From?

"Gordon!" Shane yelled. He rushed over to Gordon, who covered his nose.

"My face! My face!" Gordon moaned. "Oh, I'm dying." He fell to his knees.

"What was that?" Twenty-Three asked. "Is something eating his face?"

The monsters formed a protective circle around Gordon and Shane. I crawled under Roy's legs to get a better look.

"It was a soccer ball," said Nabila. She held it up for everyone to see.

"A soccer ball?" asked Shane.

"Yeah, and it hit me right in my zit," whined Gordon. "Right in the center."

He took his hand off of his nose. A red circle covered his eyes, nose, and forehead. His recently popped zit was right at the center.

"Bull's-eye!" said Ben.

"Excusez-moi?" a small voice said. *"Avez-vous vu ma balle?"*

A young boy in a tattered pair of shorts, shoes too big for his feet, and a clean soccer jersey stood in front of us.

Everyone froze.

I wonder what he thinks about us, I thought.

"Oui," said Nabila. She walked past the monsters. They didn't move an inch. Not even Director Z knew what to do.

"We've been caught," whispered Shane.

Nabila handed the boy the soccer ball.

"Merci," he said, and ran down a path that I hadn't seen before.

As soon as he was gone, everyone—children and monsters—started chattering nervously.

"What was he saying?" Gordon said. "Was he making fun of me?"

"No, he just wanted his ball," said Nabila.

"He's the one who kicked it?" asked Gordon. "Man, I've never been hit so hard in my life."

"He didn't seem to care that a bunch of Americans were rolling through the jungle with a bunch of monsters," said Shane.

"He didn't even say anything about Roy," said Ben.

"Where *is* Roy?" I asked. I looked around.

Roy came out from behind a tree. "Sorry, I got scared."

"No, it's good that the soccer ball kid didn't see you," I said. "Twenty-Three must have been behind someone, and Clive looks pretty good—for a zombie, anyway."

"Fresh air and sea spray are totally rejuvenating," said Clive. He gave the sign for *hang ten*. "Yeah!"

"You guys stay here," I said to the monsters. "We're going to investigate."

"Yes," said Director Z. "Let's go investigate."

Director Z walked forward, but I held up my hand. "No," I said. "You're too creepy."

"Creepy?" Director Z said. "I'm not a zombie. I'm not a Bigfoot."

"You're a tall, pale adult walking through the jungle in the searing heat with a perfectly pressed suit on," I said. "You're totally creepy."

"Yeah, if there are more kids, we should be the ones to talk with them," Gordon said.

"Fine," Director Z said. "But be careful!"

We followed the path the soccer kid had taken. Giggles and shouts filled the air.

"That sounds like a lot of kids," said Nabila.

"Hopefully there are no adults with them," Ben said. "Adults are always asking too many questions. Kids just get it, you know?"

"Yeah, we should just tell them what's going on," said Shane. "The monsters, Chris's journey, the great time we had in Egypt. I'm sure they'll help."

"I'm not sure about that," I said. "Kids are better than adults, for sure, but we have to think up a cover story."

The path opened up on a clearing. We stepped out onto a crude soccer field.

WHOOOOOOSH.

A soccer ball flew past the tip of my nose. Shane snatched it before it smashed him in the face.

"Catlike reflexes," said Gordon. "Wish I had those." He rubbed his zit again.

A few kids ran up to us. The rest stayed on the field, annoyed that their game had been interrupted.

"*Parlez-vous anglais?*" asked Nabila.

"Huh?" said Gordon.

"*Oui*," said one of the older kids. "I mean, yes! Where are you from?" He also wore a clean soccer jersey, but his big toe was poking out of the front of a very old shoe.

"We're from America," Nabila said. "Well, I'm from Egypt, but they're from America."

"What are you doing here?" he asked.

Shane blurted out, "We were trapped in an Egyptian pyramid after an old friend went a little cuckoo, and now we and the monsters that helped save us are helping Chris here, who's currently suffering from a brain fever and had to eat an armpit raisin."

"*Quoi?*" the kid asked.

"He doesn't understand," said Nabila.

"Hiking," I yelled quickly before Shane could say anything else. "We're going hiking."

"Ah, hiking," he said. "*Je comprends*. Why are you hiking here?"

"School trip," I said.

"I understand," he said. "What's your name?"

"Chris," I said. "What's yours?"

"Diblo," he said. "You like to play soccer?"

"Yeah, totally!" yelled Gordon. He rushed out on the field.

A little kid grabbed the ball from Shane and threw it out after Gordon. Everyone followed.

"Wait, Diblo!" I yelled. "I want to ask you. Does anything strange ever happen in this town? You know, scary stuff? I like to write stories, and I'm always looking for ideas."

"We got plenty of scary old people here," said Diblo. "They scare women who walk out late. They eat all the chickens."

"Tell me more," I said.

"A friend, he sees one out late at night," Diblo said. He laughed. "The person was so old, my friend scared him! No eat chickens that night!"

"Old?" asked Shane. "Old . . . monsters?"

"Who knows, could just be crazy," said Diblo. "We always had a few old crazies like that. Retirement home outside of town for rich old crazies. Fly in from all over the world. And the rest of us want to be anywhere but here."

"A retirement home, huh?" I said.

Gordon ran back up to us. "Guys, you've got to get in on this game," he said. "They're awesome! They'd destroy the Rio Vista team—and we've won finals three years running."

Diblo stared down at Gordon's feet, and his face lit up. "We even better with shoes like these. Where you get these?"

"Oh, these?" asked Gordon. "They're all right, I guess. Come on, guys, let's—"

"We need to go," I said, interrupting Gordon. "You know we have a tight hiking schedule to keep."

"Come on, man, I just got started," Gordon said.

Shane walked over to grab Gordon and dragged him back up the trail.

"Nice to meet you, Diblo!" I said.

But Diblo was just staring at Gordon's shoes.

Haunted Hiking

Back in the jungle, the monsters shuffled around restlessly as we told Director Z what Diblo had told us.

"I wonder who's living in that retirement home," Clarice said. "My old friend Betty screamed her way out of Raven Hill, and I always wondered where she went. She often talked about traveling."

"Oooh, is Betty a chicken-eater?" asked Pietro. "I wonder if she'd be interested in sharing." He licked his lips.

"I think that there are more important questions we need to answer," I said, turning to Director Z. "Like what is going on?"

"I should have realized this before," said Director Z. "You're being called to a facility."

"A facility?" Nabila asked.

"A retirement home," replied Director Z. "The signs were in front of us as we made our way here, as plain as day, but I ignored all of them. I had never heard of a retirement home in this remote location, so I never even thought it was possible."

"But Diblo must have been talking about a monster retirement home," I said. "I'm sure of it."

"Vait a minute!" yelled Grigore. "Not every crazy old person is a monster."

"No, Chris is right," said Director Z. "I'm sure now that a monster retirement home is nearby. And it's in some sort of jeopardy."

"Jeopardy?" asked Gordon. "You mean with Alex Trebek?"

"No, he means 'in trouble,'" said Nabila.

"There is an ancient rule," said Director Z, "so ancient that I had nearly forgotten it. It is a sacred oath that every Director is obligated to fulfill: If a Director is without a retirement home and there is a retirement home nearby in need, the Director must immediately proceed to that location and offer his or her assistance."

"But I never took an oath," I said.

"I was too busy to lay out all of the rules when I gave you the pendant, but you technically took the oath when you took the pendant," said Director Z. "I told you that it was a huge responsibility and figured that about covered it."

"The last thing I remember before you guys brought me back from insanity was getting the pendant from Murray," I said. "This all began right when I became a Director again."

"Yes," said Director Z, "as soon as the pendant was back in your possession, it called you here."

"What do you think is wrong with the retirement home?" asked Shane.

"There's no way to tell," said Director Z. "But we've already seen a corpse flower somewhere it shouldn't be, and the vampire boars point to some sort of chaos that's spread farther than the confines of the retirement home. Your new friend has clearly told us that residents have overrun the town."

"I don't know if they've taken over the town so much as annoyed it," said Ben.

"Well, no matter what, time's a-wastin'," said Gordon. "Now that we know what needs to be done, let's get Chris in, get out, and get HOME." He turned to rush deeper into the jungle.

Director Z reached out to stop him. "Did you not hear what I said?" asked Director Z. "It's only in very severe cases that a Director is called to a retirement home. We must proceed with caution." Director Z turned to me. "And it's going to be hardest on Chris. Whatever chaos we find there must be controlled by him. We can only help."

Without saying a word, I started walking.

"Oh, this is going to be fun!" said Shane. He took the lead with me. "This is like *Tomb Raider* or *Temple of Doom*!"

We hadn't even been walking for ten minutes when the jungle got incredibly thick. The farther we walked, the thicker it got.

"I feel like it's pushing in on us," said Gordon.

A vine reached down and grabbed Clive's shoulder. "Hey!" Clive said. "Get outta my space, man!" He ripped the vine off of his shoulder and gave it a CHOMP. The jungle shuddered all around us.

"That's not good," said Shane.

"Now it really *is* moving in on us!" yelled Ben.

The plants and trees of the jungle surrounded us. They covered us in a massive, writhing green cage so thick that we could barely see anything.

"The machetes!" yelled Director Z.

Roy pulled three machetes out of his bag. He tossed one to Grigore and one to Director Z and kept one.

Immediately, the three began hacking away at the vegetation in front of us. A small hole of light appeared.

"We're breaking through!" yelled Director Z. "Everyone get over here!"

HISSSSSSSSSSSSNO.

"Aargh!" yelled Ben. He fell to the ground.

"What is it?" Shane yelled.

We ran over to help Ben, avoiding the vines that tried to trip us like insane double Dutch ropes.

"It's now or never!" yelled Director Z. "Hurry!"

Director Z and the monsters had opened up a door-size hole.

"We can't leave Ben behind!" I yelled.

Shane rolled Ben over, and his face was covered with zits.

"Gross!" said Gordon.

"Ben, are you okay?" asked Nabila.

"Get him up!" Director Z said.

The door-size hole shrank to a window.

Shane and Gordon tried to pick Ben up.

"Don't touch me!" yelled Ben. "They hurt so bad!" He covered his face and moaned.

"Chris!" Director Z yelled. I looked up to see that the window was closing quickly.

POP POP POP *pop pop.*

I looked back down to Ben and saw snakes crawling all over his hands. He shook and rolled back onto his face. The snakes scattered.

"Oh man!" yelled Shane. "Ben! Are you okay? Did they bite you?"

Before he could answer . . .

"Whoa!" yelled Nabila as a vine picked her up off of the ground by her feet. She swung in the air above us. "Help!"

Her glasses fell off. Shane caught them, tossed them to me, and then jumped up to grab her.

But she was too high.

The vine swung her over to a huge Venus flytrap. The trap opened slowly, revealing a disgusting, mucousy mouth with razor-sharp teeth. With a great BLLAARRRRF, the flytrap spit out the bones of its last meal and reached up for Nabila.

"Guys!" screeched Nabila. "Don't just let it eat me!"

Out of nowhere, a huge bat carrying a machete in its feet swooped in and cut the vine.

"Yeah, Grigore!" yelled Gordon.

Nabila dropped just to the left of the flytrap.

"Nabila," yelled Shane. "Keep moving!"

We rushed up to help her, and the disgusting, drooly flytrap mouth came down on us just as we reached her. Its fangs were stuck in the ground on either side, and before it could free itself enough to chomp down on the four of us, I grabbed a tusk from the pile of bones it had barfed up and jabbed it into its fleshy pink leaf.

A wad of green goo squirted out, and there was a SCREEEEECH, but it continued to close its disgusting plant mouth on us. The others kicked and punched. Shane picked up another tusk.

We stabbed it again and again, but its mouth kept closing. Soon, my cheek was pressed against its sticky flesh.

"Ugh, we're going to die!" said Gordon.

"Well, we'll be digested slowly over a few days, so we have some time," said Shane.

"Don't give up," I yelled. But the Venus flytrap was squeezing us hard now.

"Can't . . . breathe . . . ," I gasped.

"They . . . aren't . . . supposed to crush . . . their prey," said Shane.

"They're . . . not . . . even native . . . to central Africa," gasped Nabila.

"Shut . . . up . . . NERDS!" gasped Gordon.

I saw stars in front of my eyes.

"Watch out!" a muffled voice said.

"For . . . what?" I gasped back.

SCHLUCK!

A machete burst through the side of the fleshy flytrap cheek a few feet in front of me. The crushing pressure stopped.

I pulled in a huge breath and screamed, "To the left!"

SCHLUCK!

The machete came through again . . .

. . . right in front of my face!

"YOUR left," I yelled even louder.

Two machetes sliced in and sawed down to the ground. Shane and I burst out of the flytrap. I saw a bright light through the writhing jungle ahead.

"Where's Ben?" I asked.

"Keep running!" yelled Director Z.

Everyone pushed through the thin layer of jungle that had been cut aside, and out into a well-manicured lawn in front of a plain, modern-looking building with no windows.

"Woohoo, we made it!" said Clive. "Ride the green wave!"

The jungle slowly quieted down until there was nothing but the sound of our heavy breathing.

"Where . . . is . . . Ben?" I gasped. "This is the place." I fell over onto my side.

Roy walked over to me with Ben in his arms.

"I'm here," said Ben. "I'm okay, Roy. You can put me down. Thank you."

"Your face doesn't look okay," said Gordon. "What happened back there?"

Roy put Ben down, collected the machetes, and put them back in his massive bag.

"I have no idea," said Ben. "I hadn't had a zit in my life until five minutes ago, and now I've just had five pop at once."

"Yeah, I heard all the popping," I said. "And then I saw snakes all over your hands. How did they get there so fast? You don't think—"

"Aw, man!" Shane yelled. He looked up to the building with disappointment. "I was hoping for *Tomb Raider*, and I got my dentist's office."

Director Z walked up to the front door. "Are we ready? Let's see what this place has in store."

He pressed the buzzer on the door, but nothing happened. He put his hand on the doorknob and . . .

"Boss, watch out!" yelled Gil.

But it was too late. A huge metal arm came out from above the door and quickly wrapped its claw around Director Z's throat.

Is Anybody Home?

Director Z turned silent . . . and blue.

"Director Z!" Ben shouted. "Somebody do something!"

Roy ran up to the mechanical arm and tugged on either side of the claw with all of his might.

GRRRRWWWWAAAAAH!

"You're not moving it at all," said Nabila.

I ran up to see if there was something—ANYTHING—that I could do.

I looked at the arm, desperate to find a switch.

"I am your Director!" I yelled. I pulled out my pendant and waved it around, hoping something would

happen. Director Z's eyes bulged out of his head.

My monkey friend appeared from nowhere, jumped up onto my shoulder, and started going nuts.

EEEEEEEK!

"Ah, get off of me, you crazy thing!" I tried to tear it off of my shoulder, but it held on tightly and pointed at the buzzer on the door.

I looked and saw what the monkey had been squeaking about: a small groove under the buzzer.

I shoved my pendant into the groove, and the door swung wide open into darkness.

The claw dropped Director Z. Roy caught him, and the others came over.

"You're one smart monkey," I said. "Loud and annoying, but smart."

"Director Z still looks pretty gnarly," said Clive.

"Boss," said Pietro. He slapped Director Z's cheeks. "Boss?"

Director Z's face remained blue and his hands stayed motionless.

"Somebody's going to have to do mouth-to-mouth!" said Pietro.

"Burpcessitation?" asked Shane. He looked at me, waiting for the answer.

"No, please," gasped Director Z. "No more burpcessitation!" He jumped out of Roy's arms. He still looked a little bug-eyed as he COUGH COUGH

COUGHed and rubbed his neck, but he was okay.

I pulled the pendant out of the groove next to the door, but the door stayed open.

"I figured if it could possess me to come to this facility, the least it could do was protect everyone I'm traveling with," I said. "Now look at what's happened to Director Z. What good is the power if I can't use it?"

"Well, in the end, if it weren't for the pendant, Director Z would be dead," Shane said. "You literally hold the key to this place."

Gordon peeked through the door into the darkness. "Is anybody home?"

HOME OME OME UM UM MM MM . . .

Gordon's voice echoed through the cold, dark facility. There was no response.

"I'm surprised it's empty," said Director Z. He looked like his pale self again and adjusted his crisp suit. "They must have left in a hurry to forget to turn off such stringent security measures."

"Do you think there will be any *more* security measures?" asked Gordon.

"Possibly," Director Z responded. "Roy, would you mind taking the lead?"

"Oh, come on, Boss!" whined Roy.

"DO IT," Director Z commanded.

"Fine," mumbled Roy, and he headed into the facility.

We followed.

Gordon flicked a switch on the wall on and off, but nothing happened.

I let my eyes adjust to the little light that came through the door, and then looked around. "It's just as drab on the inside as it is on the outside."

"I'm getting some strange smells," said Pietro.

"Tell me something I don't know," Ben said.

Roy walked down a dark hallway.

"Wait, Roy," said Shane. "Not all of us can see in the dark. Can you bust out the flashlights?"

Roy shuffled back and handed out the three flashlights that were in his bag. Then he pulled out a lantern and went down the hallway once again. The light sent strange shadows up on the walls.

"Is that blood?" asked Nabila. She shone her flashlight on the wall.

"I'm afraid so," said Director Z.

"It's fresh," said Pietro.

"How fresh?" Shane asked.

Pietro stuck out his tongue and was just about to lick the red stain on the wall when—

"Bad dog!" yelled Director Z. "Don't lick that blood. It could turn you into a gruesome jungle monster."

Pietro growled and moved away from the wall.

We peeked into room after room. A dining room with rotting food. Sitting rooms with ripped-up leather couches. Bedrooms with furniture on the ceiling.

We walked into a research library. It was filled with everything from stone tablets to electronic tablets. Most of the books had spilled out of the bookcases.

"What a mess," said Ben. He walked up to one of the few books still standing on the shelf and pulled it off.

SCCCRRAAAPPEGRIND!

"Whoa!" yelled Ben, jumping back.

The bookcase swung open, and a corpse fell out of the wall onto Ben.

"Get it off me!" yelled Ben. He was pinned. The body jiggled and shook, and its clothes began to bulge.

A cobra burst out of the neck of the corpse, reared up, and hissed at Ben.

"That poor zombie," said Clarice.

"Poor zombie?!" Ben said, staring the cobra in the eyes. "How about poor *me*? Someone do something! Should I move? Should I look away?"

Before the cobra could strike, Roy rolled the corpse off of Ben.

The corpse shook like crazy as snakes burst out of every body part, leaving a trail of blood and guts as they slithered out of the room.

"Uh, hey, guys," Shane said to the snakes as they slithered away. "Do you live here?"

"I don't think anyone is left," said Director Z, scratching his chin mysteriously.

"Does that mean I'm free?" I asked Director Z.

Before Director Z could answer, there was a large BANG from the next room.

We all froze.

BANG BANG BANG.

Grigore moved down the hall and peeked into the room. "There's something in the laboratory," he said. "Or, rather, there's something that vants to get out."

BANG SHUFFLE BANG.

"Roy, we might need your muscle," said Director Z.

"Aw, Boss!" Roy whined.

BANG BANG BANG.

"Just do it!" yelled Director Z.

We all slowly crept into the laboratory. It smelled like a rotten hospital. Jars lined the stainless steel shelves. Some were filled with strange specimens. Others had spilled their contents onto the floor.

"Is that an arm on the examining table?" asked Ben.

I shone my flashlight on the table, and the hand on the arm gave a thumbs-up.

BANG BANG BANG.

There was a door in the back of the laboratory.

Director Z knocked on the door and said, "Whoever is in there, we're here to help you."

BANG SHUFFLE BANG GROWL.

"Please, your new Director has arrived," Director Z continued. "Show some decorum."

"What are we going to do?" asked Nabila.

"We've got to open the door and hope we can control whoever is in there," replied Director Z. "Ready?"

Roy and Grigore stood in front of the door. Pietro turned into a werewolf and raised his hackles. The monkey on my shoulder began to chatter nervously.

"You're going to make me deaf," I told the monkey.

"Maybe we should head to another room?" asked Ben.

"One . . . two . . . ," Director Z counted, "THREE!"

A flash of light blasted our eyes as Director Z opened the door. A small dark figure charged between Roy's legs, directly at Shane.

"Watch out!" Roy yelled.

But Shane was blinded by the light. He had no idea something was headed his way.

A Nice Place to Retire

The little brown creature ran right at Shane—and through his legs!

"It's another boar!" yelled Pietro.

"A vampire boar?" asked Ben.

It ran into the dark lab, SQUEEEEEEEEING the whole way.

"I don't think so," said Director Z.

"Looks like the vampires forgot a snack," said Gordon.

"How did it get in?" asked Nabila.

Roy stuck his head into the bright room and pointed at the wall in the back.

"Through there," he said.

There was a massive hole in the wall. Through the wall I could see blue skies and more jungle.

"I wish I had known about this entrance to the facility earlier," said Director Z. He rubbed his sore neck.

We walked into the room. The ceilings were twice as high as any room we had seen in the retirement home. I turned and saw a huge, empty glass water tank next to a twenty-foot-tall robot.

The sun that came through the hole shone off its well-polished, silvery metal.

"That thing is massive!" yelled Gordon. "Awesome!"

We walked over to get a closer look. We looked up, waiting for something to happen.

"It's not polite to stare," Shane said to the robot. "So, do you have anything to tell us?"

The robot kept on staring. I looked into its glass eyes, and thought I could see the back of its metal head.

The monkey chattered excitedly and jumped from my shoulder to one of the hands.

"Careful, little guy," said Ben. "It looks like it could crush you."

"I wonder how we turn it on?" said Gordon.

"Would you want to if we could?" asked Nabila. She walked around the robot, looking it up and down. "I can't seem to find any controls."

"It *must* work," said Gordon, getting even more

excited. "I mean, it totally made the hole in the wall, right?"

Director Z walked over to the wall and plucked a sharp white object out of the bricks that had tumbled to the ground.

"Is that a fang?" asked Gordon.

"I believe so," said Director Z. "I think it was left by whatever broke out of here."

Director Z eyed the tank suspiciously. He walked over and peered inside.

"There's another fang in there," he said. "I believe whatever used to be in that tank made the hole in the wall."

"Look," said Nabila. "There's a river right over there!"

Past a few lawn chairs and a croquet set on a wide field of grass, a river ran past us.

"Here, Fishy Fishy!" Shane yelled out to the river.

A bird squawked in the distance.

"It would appear that everyone has abandoned this retirement home," said Director Z.

"But we know they're still *somewhere*," I said. "And I still feel like we're close. I just don't know where to look. Maybe we need to ask Diblo for more clues."

The small monkey jumped off of my shoulder, screeched, and pointed out at the hole in the wall.

"Yes, yes, we know they went that way," I said.

"Pietro, do you think you can smell where they are now?"

Pietro, still a wolf, ran up to the hole and took a big long SNIFFFFF with his wet dog nose. He pawed over to me and shook his head.

Again, the monkey pointed out at the hole in the wall and screeched.

"I'm getting sick of this little guy," said Gordon.

"*You're* getting sick of him?" I asked. "Has he been breathing down *your* neck this whole time? I think he pooped down my back."

Shane came over to have a look. "Nope," he said. "Just Venus flytrap guts. You must have gotten them on you when you stabbed the killer plant."

EEEEEEEK! EEEEEEEEEEE!

"Go on, monkey, go perch on Gordon," I said.

"Wait, it's pointing at something!" said Ben. "Look!"

I looked where Ben was pointing, and that's when I saw it. Shane saw it, too.

"Awesome," Shane said. "I knew we'd find someplace right out of *Tomb Raider*!"

On the shore upriver from us stood a huge stone ruin. It was so covered in jungle vegetation that I hadn't even noticed it before.

"That looks like a nice place to retire," said Clarice.

"Yes," I said confidently. "Yes. That's where they're hiding out."

"I can't take much more of this jungle stuff," said

Gordon. "I like it better in this clean facility."

"I don't really think I'd call it clean," said Nabila. "Unless you don't mind the blood on the walls and the boars running wild."

"All I'm saying is, I saw a shower back in one of the rooms," Gordon said. "And I could really use one. I've got to wash my greasy face. Look, I have another zit popping up right on the tip of my nose."

"I could really use a manicure, now that you mention it," said Grigore. He inspected his long, dirty nails. "My cuticles are a mess."

"We don't have any time for showers or manicures," I said. "It's going to be sunset soon, and who knows what we're going to have to fight to get into that place—I'd rather do it during the day."

"All right, you heard the man," said Shane, pretending to be a drill sergeant. "Let's get moving." He marched through the hole.

The hole was so large that we could go through two by two. The cool dark of the facility gave way to the heat of the open field.

I reached up to my shoulder and realized the monkey hadn't jumped back on.

I peered back in through the hole and saw the monkey climbing on the robot.

"Come on," I said. "You don't have time to play with the robot."

It howled in disappointment and then joined the rest of us out in the sun.

"Oh man, I think I'm going to melt," said Ben. "Where's the shady jungle when you need it?"

"At least we can see what's creeping up on us," said Shane. "Which right now seems to be a whole lot of nothing."

"There are a lot of holes out here, though," said Gordon. "What's that all about?"

"Zombie meerkats?" asked Nabila.

"Watch your ankles, people!" yelled Shane, still in the lead.

We made it to the edge of the plain. The ruins loomed ahead of us in the jungle, tucked right up against the river. The old black stones seemed impenetrable. The trees were lined with huge bats that hung upside down like giant furry fruit.

"Something tells me they're not going to want to let us pass," said Shane.

"Let me go talk vith them," said Grigore, and with a POP, he turned into a bat.

He approached a smaller group of bats with a SQUEAK. Almost immediately, the bats stretched out their wings and swooped at him.

"They're at least five times his size!" said Shane. He cupped his hands around his mouth yelled, "Grigore, get back here!"

Grigore didn't need to be told twice. He ducked two attacks and then POPPED back into human form about ten feet off of the ground.

FWAP.

He hit the ground and bounced a few times. His forehead bled terribly.

"Were you bitten?" asked Pietro as he ran up to him. "Are you going to become a double-vampire?"

"There isn't such a thing, and they veren't vampires," said Grigore. "They vere fruit bats. It's strange that they're being so aggressive. They're usually pretty friendly. It's like something's possessing them."

"Can you negotiate with them?" asked Director Z.

"Vhat do you think I vas doing up there?" asked Grigore, frustrated. "Asking vhat time it vas?"

"I'm sorry, old man," said Director Z. He pulled a white handkerchief out of his pocket and began to dab at Grigore's head.

"Save that rag for later," said Grigore. "It'll make a nice snack vonce it's dried out."

"Mmmm, blood jerky," said Gordon.

"Maybe we could swim up the river a bit and then come up to the other side of the ruin," I suggested.

"What about Fishy Fishy?" asked Shane.

"You're right," I said. "Ugh! If these monsters really want me to help them, they should make it a little bit easier!" I kicked the ground in frustration and got my foot caught in one of the many holes. "Stupid holes!"

I had to sit down on my rump in order to pull my leg out of the hole. When I did, I saw how deep it went.

A lightbulb went off in my head.

"Twenty-Three," I said, "I need your help. Are you up for a special mission?"

"Always!" he said, and scampered over to my side. "What is it?"

"I want you to crawl deep into this series of meerkat tunnels and see if one leads to the ruin," I said.

"Even if one doesn't, I'm sure I could find the closest one and dig the rest of my way there," he replied. "I'll do it!"

He quickly jumped into the hole that my foot had gotten stuck in.

"Wait!" I said. "Once you get there, you've got to convince the monsters in the ruins to let us past the bats."

"Tell them residents are seeking shelter," said Director Z. "They can't say no to that. Don't mention that Chris is a Director."

"Got it," said Twenty-Three.

Twenty-Three disappeared under the ground.

We waited.

No Turning Back

It had been a whole hour since Twenty-Three had headed underground, and the sun had almost set on yet another crazy jungle day.

"Maybe I should turn into a mist and try to float past the bats," said Grigore.

"Why didn't you think of that before?" I said. "Twenty-Three is probably still clawing at a rock and getting nowhere. Can you turn into a rat and see how he's doing?"

"No need," said Twenty-Three. He walked out from the jungle under the fruit bats.

Behind him, the jungle shook and shimmied, and a

huge fruit bat the size of a professional football player walked through the green, his wings wide open in welcome.

"My friends!" he said. "It's so nice to have you here. I'm sorry that my cousins kept you from approaching. They usually only do that to humans. Any humans here today?"

Shane was about to say something, but Director Z motioned for him to *zip it*.

"All right, then!" said Fruit Bat Man. "Come on inside. My name's François, and I'm one of the few of us up during the daytime. I keep watch over my cousins. Many of the residents are finishing their afternoon naps in preparation for another night on the town. Our leader, Tikoloshe, is too busy to meet with you right now, but I'm sure he'll be happy to know our numbers have grown once again."

"Do your numbers grow often?" asked Shane.

"Oh, yes," said François. "We have new residents arrive from all over the world every month. But we have plenty of space—there's still an entire wing of our new home that could be used. But who is here . . . hmmm . . . aside from our African residents—Mokele-mbembe, Kongamato, a few adzes, and many more—Rangda is here from Bali, we have a banshee from America—"

"Betty," screeched Clarice excitedly.

"—a penanggalan from Malaysia, various European

vampires and werewolves, a handful of zombies from South America . . ."

François continued his list as we walked up the massive stairs of the ruin into the main section of the building. He swung open a huge wooden door that creaked on rusty hinges. Inside, it was cool and inviting.

"Enter, please," said François. "The others should be up to meet you shortly."

"Now that we're here," I said, "there's something I need to tell you."

"Oh, I know," said François. "You children are human, aren't you? It took me a while to figure out, because these two look like zombies, with those terrible head wounds." He pointed at Gordon and Ben.

"Hey!" said Gordon. "They're just zits."

"You certainly don't look like the children from town," said François. "Not that they'd be stupid enough to come here, anyway." He turned to the monsters and Director Z. "Have you brought us a present?" he asked. "A little something to munch on?"

"A present, yes," said Director Z. "But it's not what you think."

"I'm your new Director," I said.

François threw back his head and laughed so hard a brick jiggled out of the ceiling and almost smooshed Twenty-Three.

"No, really," I said. I held up my pendant. "Look."

"We already have a Director," said François. "Tikoloshe is our Director."

"I'm sorry, Teek-oh-what?" asked Gordon.

"We don't need you," said François. "We don't want you. Tikoloshe will make us strong. Tikoloshe has plans for us. He's already given us freedom we never had at the old facility. We can run free and be who we want to be."

My cheeks turned red with anger. We had come this far only to be laughed at and told off.

"Fine," I said. "I came all this way to help you out, and you're going to turn that help down? Fine by me. I'm outta here!"

I walked back down the stairs. After the third step, a white light filled my eyes, and my head split open with pain. I tumbled down to the bottom of the stairs, knocking the monkey off of my shoulder.

"Chris," said Shane. "Are you okay?" He ran down to help me back up the stairs. The monkey followed.

"Just give me more armpit raisins," I said to Gil. "Let me clear my head."

"I told you," said Director Z. "You have made a sacred oath. If you break that oath, dire consequences will ensue."

"Can't I take Gallow Manor, and you take whatever this place is?" I asked.

"It doesn't work that way," said Director Z. "Now

that you're here, you have to bring this retirement home to order. Only then will you be able to walk out of its doors. But you'll have to return if you're gone too long. You and this place are now forever connected."

I couldn't believe what Director Z said. How could I stay in this place forever? But before I could say anything, Director Z turned to François. "You have to let the children stay here," he said.

"We have to do nothing," said François. "Now get out of here."

He picked me up and brought me to the door. My head exploded again.

"Argh!" I yelled. "It hurts! My brains are turning to liquid."

"You can't let him suffer like this." Roy stepped forward.

"What do I care if your young friend suffers?" asked François. "He's only a child, not one of us!"

The stars in my eyes were now blindingly bright. I felt like I was going to throw up my brain.

"What do you care if we take up the abandoned wing?" asked Nabila. "You said yourself that you have space to spare. And you know that having young children around will boost your monstrous powers."

François walked back through the doorway. I was finally able to breathe again.

"True," said François. "But why have a snack of

power when Tikoloshe will soon bring us a feast?"

François headed for the door again.

"Wait," I shouted. The sound of my own voice almost made me pass out, but I continued. "If Tikoloshe has the power to help you, why hasn't he done it yet?"

François finally stopped. A puzzled look came over his face, and for the first time, it looked like he was questioning something. He threw me to the ground.

"Fine, stay if you like," he grumbled at me. "But don't expect any special treatment, and don't you *dare* even think about giving us any kind of orders."

He walked over to Roy and the others.

"As for my monster brethren," he continued, "I shouldn't have been so rude. Please make yourselves at home. It's not a lot, but it's better than the sterile facilities you first found yourselves in." He put his arm around Roy's shoulders. "You'll absolutely love our tarantula beds. They're so fuzzy and warm."

"Oh, that's okay." Roy gulped. "I'm happy to sleep on the ground."

"As you wish," said François. "Now let's go meet the others."

The House of Eternal Rest

The door slowly creaked to a close.

BANG.

"Welcome to The House of Eternal Rest!" said François.

"You can check in, but you'll never check out," I mumbled.

"We're gonna figure this out," Shane said. "How's your head?"

"Better, now that I'm inside," I said.

François led us through the entryway. It seemed eerily quiet without the chatter of bugs and squawks of birds and monkeys. Even the monkey on my shoulder stayed quiet.

"It's actually not as dreary in here as I thought it would be," said Ben. "Only mildly mildewy. Nice and cool."

"Only slightly drafty," said Nabila.

"High ceilings, plenty of natural light," said Shane.

"We're still working on the natural-light issue," said François. "The residents have been complaining. The only good thing about our previous facility was the fact that it was completely sealed off from sunlight."

Suddenly, a dark figure dropped from the massive skylight in the center of the huge room. The room went dark, and there was a blast of cold air.

WHOOOOSH!

"Duck!" yelled Shane.

A massive, leathery creature flew down toward us.

SQUUUUUUUUAK!

My friends and I hit the floor. The monkey grabbed my head so hard, I thought my skull was going to crack. I moved his wrinkly little hand from my eye and saw Director Z and the monsters staring at the winged creature in wonder. It came within inches of their faces before flying back up to the ceiling.

"Vow," said Grigore. "It's the most ancient monster I've ever seen."

"Amazing," agreed Pietro. "That wingspan must be at least fifteen feet!"

WHOOSH WHOOSH WHOOSH.

The great flaps of the creature's wings blew cool air into our faces.

"Good evening, Kongamato," said François. "Enjoy your night!"

Kongamato flapped down the hallway toward the back of the building.

We stood up and brushed the moldy dust off of our clothes. The monkey shook his fist at Kongamato.

"Was that a pterosaur?" asked Ben.

"Some would say so," said François. "Others might call him a hairless bat or bird—though I wouldn't. We have a few other mysterious creatures like him—though they are all land-based."

"Dinosaurs?" Shane said. "So this is *Tomb Raider* AND *Jurassic Park*?"

"Not exactly," said François. "But close. Their ancestors were dinosaurs, and thousands of generations later, something between rhinos and cerapods, between bats and pterosaurs, roams the deepest jungles of the Congo. Monsters feared by the pygmy tribes that used to rule this land. Modern times have left very few. But they are here with us."

"Heeeeeeeeyyyyy!" A tiny voice echoed through the cavernous room. "Let us out!"

François rolled his eyes and rushed into a small room next to the massive center room.

"These guys are so impatient," François huffed.

"Which guys?" I asked. I couldn't see anything in the room but a lantern that glowed red.

François walked over to the lantern and opened it up. Three very large fireflies buzzed out of it and hovered in front of us.

"Cool," said Ben. "I've never seen a red firefly before."

He stepped up to touch one.

"I wouldn't do that if I were you," said François.

Before Ben could ask why, one of the fireflies exploded in a blast of light—

POP!

—and a crazed-looking old man appeared in front of us.

"Take that long again, François," said the old man, "and I'll break through the lantern."

"Yeah," two buzzy little voices added.

"Talking fireflies?" asked Gordon.

"Adzes!" said Grigore.

"What?" I asked.

Before Grigore could answer, the crazy old firefly man opened his mouth with a snarl. "Ooooh, François, have you brought us a treat?"

The firefly man licked his very crooked but very fangy teeth. He looked deep into Nabila's eyes.

"I'm a tasty, tasty treat!" yelled Nabila. Her arms flapped wildly, and she stumbled toward the old man.

He opened his mouth wider.

"Enough!" yelled Director Z. He stepped in front of the old man.

As soon as the old man's gaze was blocked from Nabila, she dropped like a sack of potatoes.

"I told you, don't you dare try to give any orders around here," said François.

"You told Chris that," said Director Z. "You didn't tell me. And even though this isn't my retirement home, you have to respect me."

POP! POP!

The two other fireflies flashed into crazy old humans. There was another man and a woman. They rushed over to Nabila.

"Did someone say something about a treat?" both of them said at the same time.

"I think it's best if you find a meal in the cafeteria," said François, and he led the three away from Nabila and out into the main room.

They turned as he shuffled them out, trying desperately to look into our eyes.

"Look away," said Director Z.

"What did you say they were?" I asked Grigore.

"Adzes," he replied. "Vampires from West Africa that assume the form of fireflies. When they're captured and brought into a house by a victim, they have the ability to turn into humans."

"And possess you," said Director Z, helping Nabila off the floor. She was awake but groggy.

"Are you okay?" Ben asked.

"I think so," said Nabila. "My head hurts a little."

"Wow, we're really seeing a different side of monsterdom," said Shane. "Ancient monsters, new types of vampires, burly talking bats. Everything feels so new, just like when we started at Raven Hill Retirement Home."

"Ah, those were the days," said Pietro.

"So not all Earth monsters are like this?" asked Twenty-Three.

"No," said Director Z. "But something doesn't feel right. I don't think they're supposed to be like this. Those adzes were as old as Grigore was a few months ago, but they're acting like teenagers, reckless and out of control. They're filled with a strange energy of some sort."

"I guess that's why I was called," I said.

"Friends!" yelled François from the doorway. "Come now, let's continue the tour!"

"Keep your guard up," Director Z whispered. "I don't trust François. He goes from friendly to angry to friendly again in a flash, like he's hiding something that he doesn't know how to deal with. He's out of control."

Director Z turned to the door. "We're coming!" he yelled.

I Pledge
Allegiance
to Tikoloshe

"Most of our facility—along with the residents—is deep underground," said François. "However, there was one more thing I wanted to show you upstairs."

We walked toward the back of the ruin, in the direction that the pterosaur had flown.

We passed a room with rock slabs laid out as tables. Around one table, the adzes hovered over something.

CRUNCH MUNCH MUNCH.

"That must be the cafeteria," Ben said.

At the sound of Ben's voice, the adzes' heads popped up. With a smile, one looked at Nabila. "Hello, snackie!"

Nabila shuddered.

"Don't bother the residents as they eat," said François. "Let's keep going."

We passed other rooms in the narrow, cool hallway. There was nobody but us.

The end of the hallway led to another large room like the first we had encountered just past the entryway.

"Now we know how the pterosaur exited," said Shane. "The back of the building is completely gone."

A warm jungle breeze blew into the room. Vines crept in.

Ben craned his neck to look out at the jungle, which sloped up into a small hill. "I wish I could see another dinosaur," he said.

Shane pointed up. "Perhaps you should look for a flyby," Shane said. He turned to François. "I thought you said that you had something to show us upstairs."

"There is one tower that remains," said François.

We walked to the far side of the large, open room and came to a door set in the wall. François opened the door to reveal a spiral staircase.

"Up we go," he said.

We slowly made our way up the spiral staircase. Open windows were chiseled into the stone, and no matter how high we got, still more green from the wild jungle outside crept in.

At the top of the tower was a small room that we could barely fit into.

"Did you bring us up here for the view?" asked Shane. "Because it's pretty awesome!"

"Do enjoy the view while you're here," said François. "But there's also a bit of business we need to discuss."

"Business?" I asked.

"You must bow down to the shrine of Tikoloshe and pledge your allegiance," said François. He stepped aside to reveal a small statue of a gremlin or troll with a wide grin. The statue was surrounded by candles and burning incense sticks.

"That's one ugly statue," whispered Shane.

A wind blew through the windows and made the candles flicker. The cloud of incense moved from the statue to Shane's face.

Shane coughed twice, sneezed, and then . . .

"Arrrrrgh," Shane yelled. "My nose!"

Shane doubled over in pain. His knees hit the floor. He cupped his nose, which was as red as Rudolph's, and moaned.

"Shane!" I yelled, and moved forward to help my friend.

I lifted him up by his shoulders and swung his head back.

"Oh man!" I said. "Your nose is completely covered in zits!"

"I think they're in my nostrils!" he moaned. "It hurts so bad. Make it stop."

I held Shane in my arms as he dealt with the pain.

"Move away from the shrine, worms," growled François. "Everyone must pledge allegiance."

SLAM!

The door at the top of the stairs closed.

The monsters growled. Grigore hissed. The monkey screeched.

"We bow down to no one," said Roy. He stepped up to François.

François opened his wings wide. "If it wasn't for Tikoloshe, none of us would be here! And if you don't bow down, you won't remain here long." François was about to strike when Director Z jumped in.

"Now I'm sure we'd all be happy to bow down to Tikoloshe," said Director Z, "if—"

"Boss!" yelled Pietro.

"No way," said Gordon.

Roy tried to rush François.

"Pietro, don't interrupt me," said Director Z, holding Roy back. "I was saying, if we could know more about him. Who is he? Is he your Director? How has he helped you? What has he promised? Where is your old Director?"

"Only Tikoloshe can explain himself," said François. "And he only explains himself when he wishes. For now, you must pledge allegiance or leave this place."

"Chris can't leave this place," Director Z said to the

monsters gathered in the hot tower. "We must do it."

François put down his wings, and Roy backed off.

"You first, big man," François said to Roy. "Bow down and say, 'I pledge my allegiance, my life, and my afterlife to Tikoloshe.'"

"Hey, you didn't say anything about pledging my afterlife," said Roy.

"Director Z, we don't have to do this," I said.

"We have no choice," said Director Z. "We'll discuss terms with Tikoloshe when he arrives."

Roy bowed down. "I pledge—"

"Lower," said François.

Roy bowed lower. "I—"

"Lower," said François.

"We're going to be here forever if you're going to be that picky," Director Z said to François.

"I said lower," growled François.

Roy bowed down as far as he could and then fell forward, bashing his head on the stone floor.

THUNKK!

"Ah-ha-ha!" laughed François as Roy struggled to get up. "That's perfect, just do it on your knees!"

"I pledge my allegiance, my life, and my afterlife to Tikoloshe," said Roy. He pushed his body back up off the ground and hit his head on the corner of the shrine.

WHACK!

"Yowch!" yelled Roy.

The statue fell forward onto one of the candles.

"NO!" yelled François. He snatched up the statue and patted its smoking head with his wing-claw.

"It smells like burned bat fur," said Gordon. "Whoof!"

"Hurry up, you idiots!" yelled François, slamming the statue back in place. "Pledge your allegiance and then let's get out of this tower before you ruin everything!"

Everyone took their turn as François rushed them through.

Director Z was the second-to-last to go. "I pledge my allegiance, my—"

"Fine, fine, that'll cover it," said François, waving his wing impatiently. "Next."

I stepped up, and the statue winked at me. Its cheesy grin got even bigger.

"What's going on?" I asked.

"Hurry it up!" hissed François.

My mouth got dry, and I found it hard to speak. The statue of Tikoloshe was staring right into my eyes. They burned a little. The monkey on my shoulder let out a low growl.

I bowed down so I didn't have to look at him anymore. The monkey held on to my neck as I choked out the words:

"I pledge my allegiance, my life, and my afterlife to Tikoloshe."

Have a Nice Afterlife

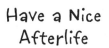

We quickly made our way down from the tower, led by François.

"Well, I for one am glad that's over," said François. He chuckled nervously and continued, "Yes, Tikoloshe is a stickler for ritual."

We passed by the smashed wall that opened into the jungle. The sun had set while we were in the tower, and now it was fully dark. The jungle was alive with the sounds of creatures of the night.

I looked over at Shane. One nostril of his nose was completely sealed shut with zits.

"Are you okay?" I asked him.

"My nose is so numb I can barely feel it now," said Shane. "But I'll be glad to finally sleep in a real bed tonight."

"What makes you think it's going to be a real bed?" asked Gordon. "I think François said something about a tarantula mattress."

"Highly recommended," François said. "It will really help with your posture. It's almost as good as hanging upside down."

We all walked up to a huge iron door I hadn't seen before.

François opened it and peeked down a set of massive stone stairs.

"Let me just prepare everyone for our new residents," said François. "I'd hate for someone to be mistaken for a snack."

As soon as François had disappeared into the darkness, I turned to Director Z.

"What did we just get ourselves into?" I asked him. "Did we really just pledge our afterlife?"

"What does that mean, anyway?" said Gordon. "Are our souls in trouble?"

"Or our complexions?" Ben asked.

"I'm not sure," Director Z responded. "But taking part in that ritual may have been worthwhile."

"How was it worth our afterlife?" Ben squeaked.

"We learned something," said Director Z. "Didn't

we, Chris?" He looked at me, waiting for me to say something.

"Uh . . . ," I stumbled.

"Think, Chris!" said Director Z. "The pendant might give you power, but your intelligence comes from within. What did we see out of the ordinary?"

"You mean, aside from the oh-so-ordinary ritual of giving our soul to a troll?" asked Gordon.

"Soul Troll," snickered Clive. "Yo. I've heard of that band."

"François freaked out when the statue hit the candle," I said.

"Yes?" asked Director Z, digging deeper. "And? What does that tell us?"

"That François is really concerned about keeping the statue safe?" I asked.

We could hear paw-steps coming up the stairs.

"Exactly," whispered Director Z. "Now think about what that means. That's what I'll be doing."

"Come on then," said François. "Everyone is excited to meet you."

We wound our way down the huge, dark spiraling staircase into the cold, deep dungeon of the ruins.

The dungeon buzzed with excitement.

"Because of all the light that filters into the top of the ruin, most of the residents start their evenings here," said François.

"I feel like we're in a pit," said Gordon.

"I love it!" said Grigore. "So homey!"

Low moans and groans floated up the stairs from below. We came down the final steps and found ourselves in a sea of old zombies, vampires, and other horrific creatures from all over the world.

"There are a lot of monsters here," I whispered. "I can't even count them all."

"Almost too many," Director Z whispered back. He rubbed his chin thoughtfully. "Like François said, they're coming from all over . . . but why?"

"But, Boss," said Grigore, "they seem so happy."

An old zombie turned to us and smiled. His jaw quickly popped off.

François bent over to pick it up. "Now," he said, "it would be best if the children slept down here at night while the residents wreaked havoc on Yangambi." He shoved the zombie's jaw back in place, and it smiled at us again.

"That's one crooked grin," said Shane.

"What's Yangambi?" I asked François.

"That's the nearby town," he responded.

"This Tikoloshe," said Director Z. "He lets you roam free in the town?"

"Like I said," said François, "Tikoloshe has given us freedom that we could only imagine before. But the residents aren't strong. They can't do too much damage.

Though I hope the chickens are restocked tonight."

"But you said that Tikoloshe was going to make you all strong," I said. "What then?"

"Well, then we'll have even more fun," said François. "The best is yet to come."

"So you'll destroy the town and kill the residents?" asked Nabila. "What about the monster code?"

François blinked at her, stared into space strangely for a moment, and then growled, "What do you know about the monster code?" He flung his wings wide open and lunged at her.

Nabila fell to the ground and covered her face. François loomed over her.

"Back off, fur ball," yelled Gordon, and he pushed François back.

"Ow," shouted François, and he fell onto the cold dungeon floor.

Gordon gave me a puzzled look. "I didn't even push him that hard."

I looked down at François, and for a moment his fur changed color from brown to gray.

"Hey, his fur is—" I started to say, but before I could finish, it had turned back to brown.

He moaned on the floor.

The other monsters began to crowd around us. They fidgeted and growled.

"Can I help you up, old man?" asked Director Z. He

reached down to help François.

"Don't touch me!" yelled François. "And I'm not old."

"No, you don't *look* old," said Director Z pointedly. "I can agree with that."

"Now, everyone, back off," said François. "I'm sorry . . . I don't know what came over me."

The monsters all growled and swayed, their old bodies forming a tight circle around us.

I helped Nabila up. Her face was covered in dozens of zits.

"Are you okay?" I asked.

"I think so," she replied. "My face feels like it's crawling with zits."

"That's because it is," I said. "Now I'm the only one who doesn't have them."

"This has got to stop," said Gordon. "All these zits are giving me more zits."

"How are you doing, Shane?" I asked. I looked over to Shane and saw the largest green booger I had ever witnessed in my life hanging from his nose. It was so big it looked like it was moving and it had eyes. I squinted to get a better look, but I couldn't tell if I was making up the eyes. It was covered in a thin layer of pus.

SNNNNNNNARF!

Shane snorted the super-pus booger back into his nose. "I'm just feeling a little congested now."

"Congested with what?" I asked. Did anyone else just see what was hanging out of Shane's nose?

Before anyone could answer, a banshee stepped forward and locked eyes with Clarice.

"Betty?" asked Clarice. "Poor old Betty, is it really you?"

Betty's eyes burned red, and she opened her mouth.

She had the sharpest teeth I had ever seen on a banshee, and started screaming as she jumped at Clarice.

Clarice screamed. The monkey screeched.

I thought my ears were going to bleed as the two banshees wrestled each other down to the floor.

EEEEEEEEEEEEEEEE!

"Clarice!!!" I yelled.

Crazy Old Friends

"Get off of me, you old bird!" yelled Clarice.

EEEEEEEEEEEEEEEE!

"Betty's screaming is making the other monsters crazy!" Ben yelled, pointing at the crowd of monsters that closed in around us. Fangs flashed. Arms reached out.

Some headed to Betty to help. Others, wide-eyed and drooling, headed for us, licking their lips.

"Snackie!" yelled a massive, hairy, tusked monster on two legs with bug eyes. "Oh, snackieeeee!!!"

"I'm sick of everyone thinking we're snack food," said Gordon. A zombie pounced on him, and he pushed

him back. Gordon turned to Clive and said, "Tell your friend to chill!"

"Sorry, dude," said Clive. "I don't speak Brazilian."

Betty and Clarice rolled around on the floor, knocking over Ben and Nabila.

"Watch out!" Nabila yelled. "Those teeth are like razors."

"Stop being such a ninny," Clarice yelled at Betty. "Get control of yourself." Clarice pulled Betty's hair, and Betty SCREEEEEEEECHed again.

The monkey screeched and pointed ahead. The tusked monster was headed right for me.

I held up my pendant and yelled, "I am your Director and I demand that you stop this instant!"

ROOOOOOOOOOOAR!

The tusked monster didn't care that I was a Director. I tried to back up, but the battling banshees were in the way.

Betty just wouldn't leave Clarice alone. Betty lifted her head, opened her toothy mouth wide, and came down on Clarice's neck.

Shane roundhouse kicked Betty in the face. She rolled off of Clarice and knocked over the tusked monster before it could sink its claws into me. I jumped to the right as Betty got up, pushed Shane to the floor, and jumped on Clarice again.

"It's all right!" screeched Clarice. "I've got this.

Watch the other ones, though. I don't trust their shifty eyes."

The younger, stronger monsters of Gallow Manor bared their fangs, bugged their eyes, and pushed back the older monsters of The House of Eternal Rest.

"I'm so confused," said Twenty-Three. "I knew Earth wasn't the most peaceful place, but I always thought monsters were supposed to help other monsters!"

"François!" I yelled. "Get up and do something before someone gets hurt!"

"I told you," said François from the safety of the floor, "you're not giving any orders around here." He wrapped his wings around his head. "I can't deal with this anymore."

"You don't want Tikoloshe to be mad at you, do you?" I asked François. "What if you hurt one of his residents?"

François stared at the battle for a second and then said, "Fine. Help me up."

Gordon and I helped François up.

He raised his wings and yelled, "Enough, everyone. It's time to head out, anyway—let's begin our night!"

But nobody listened.

"Better try harder than that, bat man," said Pietro. "These guys are getting stronger by the second."

"I . . . I . . . ," stammered François, "can't control them anymore!"

EEEEEEEEEEEEEE!

I had almost forgotten about Clarice.

She screeched the loudest she had screeched yet and lifted her hand high in the air. She made a claw and stared Betty directly in the eyes. "Enough," Clarice hissed. Her nails shone in the darkness.

EEEEEEEE-SWIPE!

"Whoa!" said Shane.

Clarice scratched Betty's face before Betty could attack with her razor-sharp teeth. Betty dropped to the floor . . .

. . . and the dungeon went deathly silent.

All of the old monsters who were struggling with my friends stopped and shuffled around aimlessly as if nothing had happened.

"That's all you got?" Gil asked the adze he had been fighting. The adze ignored him and headed up the stairs to start his night in Yangambi.

"Clarice!" yelled Betty, clutching her bloody, wrinkled face. "What did you do to me? And why are you here?"

"What am I doing?" asked Clarice, plucking the skin from under her fingernails. "What were *you* doing? It's like you were possessed."

"Well, I guess you broke the spell!" said Betty. "Come here and give an old girl a hug!"

The two banshees hugged. The rest of the monsters

shrugged and headed for the stairs.

François walked up with them. He turned at the first stair. "Well, we'll be out for the night," he said. "For your safety, I'll lock the door at the top from the outside."

"Wait, WHAT?!" Gordon screeched. "You can't do that!"

Gordon rushed at François again. This time I held him back. "What does it matter?" I said. "We know they're coming back."

I watched François carefully as he headed up the stairs.

"He looks defeated," said Nabila, walking over to me. "His wings are hanging down low. He seems tired."

"His act is wearing thin," said Director Z. "Whatever it is he's hiding, I think he's going to reveal it soon."

"We should track him," said Ben. "Keep an eye on him. Keep an eye on all of them."

Director Z motioned to Pietro.

"I'm on it," said Pietro. He jumped up the stairs and had turned into a werewolf by the time his paws hit the third stair.

"Thanks, Pietro!" I said.

"Do you think François will let Pietro join?" asked Nabila.

"François looks like he won't even notice him slink up the stairs," I said. "He probably wouldn't even notice us."

"So let's go," said Gordon. "This place is giving me the supercreeps."

"I thought you were the one who couldn't handle much more jungle," said Nabila. "And we can't leave Chris alone. Remember, he can't leave."

"Yes, stay with me," I said. "We have the secret lair of these monsters all to ourselves. Let's look for clues about this Tikoloshe. And what happened to their Director."

I turned back to the two banshees. Clarice now had a lace handkerchief in her hand and was dabbing Betty's face with it.

"Well, the good news is, it gets better from here," said Clarice. "I'm sorry that I nearly scratched your face off, but I hope it made you realize how much you need to moisturize."

"Oh, that's not going to do me any good, darling," said Betty. "Not for someone my age."

"I would have lost my mind if I didn't hold on to some piece of my youth when I was alone and sapped of all my energies," Clarice said. "I kept myself looking good and ended up kissing quite the interesting gentleman just a little while back."

"Who?" asked Betty.

Clarice simply pointed up the stairs.

"The werewolf?" gasped Betty. "My, my! I always knew you liked the hairy ones, but still . . ."

"Cut the kissy stuff," said Gordon.

"Oh, he's right, we're just gossiping," said Clarice. "Is there somewhere more private we could speak?"

"Yes, yes, what am I thinking?" Betty chuckled. "Come to my room, and I'll boil frog water for some tea."

The two ladies giggled and screeched as they made their way down the hallway.

"C'mon," I said. "Let's follow them into the hall. We can search the monsters' rooms for clues while they're all out on the town."

Slinking Around

"I've got an amazing idea," said Gordon. "How about, instead of spending so much time searching these rooms, we sleep in one of them? Not all of them have tarantula beds. This one doesn't."

"That *is* an amazing idea," said Nabila, yawning. "Being hypnotized and forced to think that you're a tasty treat is really hard work. My arms are still sore from flapping around. And my face is super sore from these zits. They're throbbing."

We stood in the center of another cell-like room deep in the dungeon of The House of Eternal Rest. A lightbulb hung from the stone ceiling, flickering.

115

Director Z and the monsters were spread out through the rest of the dungeon pawing through every room for clues that would help us get out of this mess.

"The hair all over that bed makes me think it's Rangda's," said Shane. "You know what Rangda is known for, right?"

"Rang-who?" asked Gordon, yawning.

"Rangda the Balinese witch," said Shane. "The bug-eyed tusky one that was headed for Chris when Clarice and Betty were battling. She likes to eat small children."

"Who are you callin' small?" asked Gordon.

"I'm just saying, you gotta ask yourself, 'Is Rangda feelin' hungry after a night on the town?'"

"You probably don't want your scent in any of these monsters' beds," said Nabila. "They're already ready to eat us. We don't want to keep reminding them." She stared at the mattress longingly. "Still, that looks so comfortable."

"Once we've helped Chris," Shane said, "I'm going to hunker down with some of Betty's frog-water tea and snuggle into a tarantula bed."

"Such a weirdo," said Gordon.

"Why thank you," said Shane.

"I could fall asleep standing up," I said. "My head aches and I'd love to rest, but the quicker we solve this mystery, the quicker I'm free of this place."

"That sounds like your problem," said Nabila,

yawning. "Your mystery. So tired."

I peeked under a regular mattress that wasn't made from an ever-shifting vat of tarantulas and didn't see anything but a few crumbs and centipedes. They eyed me angrily as I put it down again.

"Fine," I grumbled to Nabila. "I know you're only being a turd because your face hurts so much. Take a break here."

Nabila flopped down face-first onto Rangda's bed, and a huge cloud of hair lifted up and into the room.

SNOOOOOOOOOOOOORE.

"Wow, she really was tired," I said. "This room is clear. Nothing to find here. But let's take a breather before we head to the next one."

"What are we looking for? What is the mystery we're trying to solve?" Ben asked. "Or mysteries? There's a lot going on, and this is the first time we've stopped crashing through the jungle in three weeks."

"This is one heck of an unexplained mystery," said Gordon, probing his face while he looked into a cracked mirror. "Why is our perfect skin breaking out in volcanic zits?"

I sat on the edge of the bed, exhausted. "The zits are just one issue," I said.

"It must feel nice that you don't even have to deal with that issue," huffed Ben.

"Yet," I said back. "But I've got plenty of other things

to worry about. And I'm trying to figure out how the zits are connected to everything else. I know Director Z keeps telling me to notice things, but I've been so tired, and half the time I forget why I'm here. I mean, I didn't even know my own name until a few days ago."

"Oh, wait a minute," said Shane. He picked up a box that had been hiding under the bed, flipped it upside down, and shook it hard. "I thought this room was clear." A few moths fluttered out of the box. Shane grabbed one and pulled it up to his mouth. "But is it?"

We all waited for a reply. The moth said nothing.

Shane let the moth go and then turned to me. "Let's think this through. You were called here, as if this place were in danger. But then, when you got here, you were told that you were not needed and that Tikoloshe was here."

"I'm following so far," said Ben. "Except for the Tikoloshe part. Is he the Director?"

"I don't think he can be," I said. "Or I'd be able to leave this place."

"Unless he's such a bad Director, your pendant wants you to take over," said Gordon.

"Like he was their Director and then he went bad or something like that?" Ben asked.

"Maybe," I said. "Or maybe Tikoloshe ate the Director, and is now in charge of the monsters, but the pendant called me here because the facility still needs a

Director, even though nobody here wants one."

"Okay," said Shane. "So I think the first thing we're looking for is some scoop on Tikoloshe. That might help us figure out if he's the Director, and if not, we can keep digging from there. Plus, I think he may have something to do with our zit plague."

"You make it sound so easy," I said. "But how do we start?"

"Well, none of the other monsters trust or even care about us," said Shane, "but I bet you Betty might have some tasty gossip she'd be willing to share now that Clarice has slapped the crazy out of her."

Shane rushed out of the room and down the hall.

Ben and Gordon quickly followed.

"Wait!" I said. "I know someone has to stay with Nabila, but why does it have to be me?"

Roy ambled past the room. I jumped out and grabbed him.

"EEEEEK!" he screeched. "Are you trying to frighten me to death?"

"Are you trying to wake up Nabila?" I asked. "She's in there sleeping, and I need you to guard her while I go investigate something."

"What sort of bed is it?" Roy asked, shuddering.

"It's not a tarantula bed," I said. I shoved Roy into the room. "It's a regular old bed. Now get in there and keep an eye on her."

Stop, That Tickles!

By the time I found my way to Betty's room, Shane was already busy grilling her.

"You really can't remember anything about how Tikoloshe got here?" Shane asked.

"I'm telling you the truth," Betty said, "I can barely remember anything about him. I just have a warm fuzzy feeling about Mr. Tikoloshe. I mean, *had* a warm fuzzy feeling about him."

"What else?" I asked. "Can you remember anything? There has to be someone who knew about Tikoloshe before he came here. Maybe we could find a diary or something?"

120

"Paper?" scoffed Betty. "We're all-electronic around here."

She sipped her frog-water tea.

"All-electronic?" I scoffed back. "Really? Then what technology are you old farts using?"

"Hmmm, let me think," said Betty. She scratched her hairy chin. "I know a number of residents are on Twitter. I think I remember Rangda bragging that her handle was @tikoloshefan. It kind of makes me jealous, since I love Tikoloshe. I mean *loved,* of course. In any case, you can start with Rangda's account."

"@tikoloshefan?" Gordon asked Shane. "Rangda has an account called @tikoloshefan? So weird."

"I think a more important question is, how are you all able to charge your cell phones?" said Shane. "I could use some juice. I'd love to catch up with my friends."

"We're all here," said Gordon.

"Oh, right," said Shane.

"I wonder what Rangda was tweeting about," I said. "It's too bad we didn't find a phone in her room."

"Any phone with Twitter will do," said Ben. "It doesn't have to be hers."

"I don't actually have a smartphone," said Betty. "My cell phone's from the very early aughts. But I think Gilberto, the Brazilian zombie, always leaves his phone at home when he's out. See if you can find it in his room. It's the one with the largest tarantula bed."

"Of *course* it is," said Gordon.

We ran down the hall and found Gilberto's room.

A king-size antique claw-foot tub in the center of the room overflowed with tarantulas. Some of them crawled slowly back up the porcelain sides to join their friends. Some skittered past us and out of the door.

"I can't imagine how that's comfortable," said Gordon. "If they were all dead, maybe."

"Mmmmm," said Ben. "Rotten spider bed."

"I bet the best part is snuggling into all of their fuzz and being wrapped in their warmth," said Shane. He started to crawl into the tub.

"Stop!" yelled Ben. He pulled Shane back.

"You can nap later if you really want to," I said. "First, let's find Gilberto's cell phone."

Shane opened all of the bureau drawers. "Nothing."

Gordon rummaged through a small desk. "No smartphone here," he said.

Ben quickly peered under the tub, avoiding the spiders that dangled off the edge. "Nothing here."

"Let me go tell the others what we know so far," I said. "Keep looking in here. I'll be right back."

I walked down the hallway and didn't get that far before I heard giggling in a nearby room. I turned to have a peek and saw Twenty-Three, Gil, Grigore, Clarice, and Betty in a high cave. A strange glow came down from a hole in the ceiling.

"Did you find a clue?" I asked. "Something to do with the Director?"

"The moon is so beautiful," said Twenty-Three. "Wow, I lived on such a beautiful thing. Thank you for showing us."

They all stared up, but their eyes were glazed over.

"Guys, are you talking with someone?" I asked.

None of them answered, so I looked up with them. A small shadowy figure was peering down through the large hole. I couldn't tell what it was because the moon was so bright.

"Who is that?" I yelled up, and with the wave of a hand, the shadowy figure disappeared.

My face tightened and felt funny. I reached up and felt a bump on my nose. Two bumps on my forehead. A few more on my cheeks.

I turned to my friends, who were still staring up at the moon.

"Guys?" I asked.

They kept staring.

"GUYS, look at me!" I said. "Can you tell me if I have zits on my face? It feels so weird."

They all finally lowered their heads and looked at me. "Oh, I didn't see you there," said Gil. "Hi, Chris. Isn't the moon beautiful?"

"I've been standing here for, like, two minutes," I said to Gil.

They all stared at me.

"Okay, so tell me what you see," I said.

They kept staring at me.

"Guys, stop it, you're freaking me out," I said.

Grigore smiled a very toothy smile and stared into my eyes. I was frozen.

"Grigore, stop it!" I yelled. "Just tell me how bad these zits look and then look away."

Grigore opened his mouth, and his fangs grew.

"Chris! Chris!" Ben yelled, and ran into the room. Grigore dropped his gaze, and I was able to turn around.

"What is it?" I asked.

Ben jumped at the sight of my face.

"Oh, you finally got the zits, huh?" he asked. "We found the phone. It's in the bed."

"In the bed?" I asked. "With the tarantulas?"

"Yes, and Shane wants to jump in and grab it," Ben said. "Hurry!"

The monsters and I rushed into the other room. Shane was on the lip of the bathtub looking down.

"I just saw it, three or four spiders deep," said Shane. "This is going to be so awesome."

"Are you really sure you want to do that?" I asked.

"Awww, yeah," he said, and jumped in. The spiders stopped moving, and he lay there for a minute, enjoying the back-soothing comfort of the world's greatest, but most bizarre, mattress.

"They've locked into place," I said. "How are you going to get it?"

"Lemme see," he said, and began to slide his hand into the mass of spiders. They shifted around uncomfortably. "Aaah, that tickles!"

TEE HEE HEE HEE!

I looked over at Grigore. He looked back at me and furrowed his brow. "Vhat?" he asked.

Shane pushed his arm elbow-deep into the spider mattress and concentrated. "I thought it was right here."

"Twenty-Three, do you want to help Shane?" I asked.

"No, no, I got this!" said Shane.

That's when the other spiders grabbed his left arm and pulled it in.

"Wait, wait!" yelled Shane. But the spiders pulled hard, and Shane's face smooshed up against the pile. "SNOP IT! SNO—"

And then his head was under the tarantulas.

Tweeting with Tarantulas

"Help him, guys!" I shouted.

The monsters jumped up to the bed as Shane was pulled headfirst into the writhing mass of spiders.

Grigore and Twenty-Three jumped in first, but were stuck on top. The tarantulas wouldn't let them in deep enough to help Shane.

"Claw them all out!" I yelled. Grigore and Twenty-Three knelt down and began to claw furiously at the pile, but only a few tarantulas flew off the side of the tub.

"Shane!" yelled Ben. "I told you that you shouldn't have done this!"

"All right, everyone in!" I said.

But before anyone else could get on the tarantula bed-tub, Shane rose to the surface, giggling. "Oh man, this tickles, but it's amazing!" He pulled up one hand, which was clutching a smartphone. He tossed it to me. "Here ya go."

Grigore and Twenty-Three jumped off of the bed.

Shane backstroked through the tarantulas. "Aw, man, I knew it would be perfectly snuggly and warm in here. What I didn't think was that they'd help me find the phone."

"And your zits are gone, too," said Gordon.

"Are they really?" asked Shane. "Bonus! One of the tarantulas must have sucked them dry."

HWURRRP!

Ben threw up in his mouth a little. He swallowed hard and said, "Congratulations."

I looked down at the phone in my hand. It had a skull and crossbones logo over the word "iGroan."

"An iGroan?" asked Ben. "That's pretty funny. Does it work like an iPhone?"

My friends and the monsters crowded around me as I turned on the phone.

"Here's Twitter," I said. I clicked on the app.

"It looks like his handle is @aaaarnnnnggg," I said.

"Not very original for a zombie, if you ask me," Ben said.

"What's he tweeting about?" asked Gordon.

"His last tweet is from a few months ago," I said. "It was 'wwwwrrrrgggggnnnnn.'"

"Not so helpful," Gil said. "Zombies are terrible tweeters."

"I bet you if Clive tweeted, he'd be great at it," Shane said from the bed.

"Search for '@tikoloshefan,'" said Gordon.

"Found it," I said. "'Rangda from Bali is Tikoloshe's Number One Fan and—'"

"Just get to her tweets," said Ben.

"'I'm so glad Tikoloshe took over instead of just helping. @bettyfrancois was just terrible,'" I read.

"Wait," said Ben. "@bettyfrancois? Betty and François are a couple?"

"Sorry, it's @BATTYfrancois," I said.

"Oh, that makes sense," said Ben. "So is François the Director? Why did Tikoloshe need to help? How did he take over?"

"I'm not sure," I said. "All of Rangda's tweets are about how great Tikoloshe is." I loaded a picture and pointed at the screen. "Look, here's a selfie of her and Tikoloshe."

"She really is Tikoloshe's Number One Fan," said Ben.

"Man, he's even uglier than his statue," said Gordon.

"Does he have a Twitter account?" asked Ben.

"It doesn't look like it, but let me see who Rangda follows," I said.

"Jeez, almost everyone is here," I said. "It looks like Betty and the adzes are the only ones not on here."

"Even Kongamato?" Shane asked from the bed. "How does he even tweet with his huge wings?"

"Yeah, he's here," I said. "@realkongamato. Maybe someone does it for him?"

"What is he tweeting about?" asked Shane.

"He hasn't tweeted in a while," I said. "The last thing on here is that @battyfrancois, to help his residents regain their monster juice, is going to call on Tikoloshe for help and energy."

"So François was worried about his residents, called on this guy, and then ended up being taken over," Ben said. "So, technically, this retirement home is without a Director."

"Can't François just take control?" I asked. "Why am I here? This is someone else's mess!"

"Is anyone tweeting about zits?" asked Shane. "Check for the hashtag #zits."

"Nobody Rangda is following is tweeting about zits," I said.

"Can you Google 'Tikoloshe'?" asked Ben. "What sort of a monster is he?"

Everyone quieted down while I did a little bit of research.

"He's found mainly in South Africa," I said. "Some say he's invisible. All say he can possess people and trick them into doing things."

I thought about it for a minute. Each time something strange had happened here, it was as if the monster had been possessed.

"So that's who you were talking to in the cave," I said to the monsters. "He's trying to get you on his side, too!"

"Ve vere talking to someone?" Grigore asked.

"Well, at least I know why you tried to bite me before," I said.

"I tried to VHAT?!" asked Grigore, horrified that he might have done something wrong. He covered his mouth.

"We've got to tell Nabila about this," I said.

There was a loud chuckle coming from the large cave.

"Is that Roy?" asked Gordon. "Looks like Tikoloshe got him, too."

"If that's Roy, then who is guarding Nabila?" I asked.

Director Z rushed down the hallway with Pietro and ran into the room.

"The monsters are coming down the stairs," said Pietro.

"Clear out of their rooms immediately," added Director Z.

"Aw, man," said Shane. "I was just starting to fall asleep."

Shane jumped off of the tarantula bed. I tossed the phone back onto the impression he made. The tarantulas shifted around, and the phone disappeared again. In its place, a dead snake appeared. The tarantulas worked together to bring it to the edge of the bed and flung it on the cold stone floor.

It *plopped* like a nasty green booger.

Almost like the same booger I had seen hanging out of Shane's nose before.

The thought of a snake that big popping out of Shane's face made my stomach churn. I reached up to my own zits and felt that they were getting bigger. I thought back to the dead zombie that had fallen on Ben. All of those snakes burst from his body . . .

But there was no time for terrifying thoughts.

"We've got to get to Nabila before Rangda comes in!" I yelled.

We rushed out of the room.

Sorry Monsters

We rushed out of Gilberto's room and down the hall.

I pushed Director Z into the cave, where Roy and Clive were staring up at the moon. "Snap them out of whatever trance Tikoloshe has got them in and hurry down to Rangda's room. We might need them!"

We ran down the dark dungeon hallway. We almost knocked over Gilberto as he shuffled past us.

Shane stopped to talk with him. "I hope you don't mind, I softened up your mattress," he said. Gilberto just stared at Shane blankly.

A few doors down, Nabila screamed.

"Come on!" I huffed at Shane.

We all rushed into the room. I expected to see Rangda dining on Nabila in her bed.

Instead, more than a dozen small snakes cornered Nabila in the back of the room. She used a lighter from her fanny pack to push them back, but they weren't going far.

"Where'd they come from?" asked Ben.

"I don't know!" said Nabila. "They were here when I woke up!"

"Well, at least your zits look better," I said.

"Did you pop all of your zits?" Ben asked.

Her zits, though smaller, looked like they had just been powerfully popped. A little bit of pus and blood dripped out of one or two of them.

"I don't remember doing it," Nabila said. "How about we discuss the zits later and take care of the snakes now? OW!" She dropped the hot lighter.

The snakes slithered slowly toward her.

Pietro, in werewolf form, jumped into the room and began crushing snake heads and flinging dead snakes into the hallway with his powerful jaws.

When his task was done, he turned into a human.

"Where did those guys come from?" asked Pietro. "They taste freshly born."

"What do you mean?" Nabila asked.

Again, my stomach turned. *Did they come from her face?* I thought.

Before we could discuss the topic further, Rangda angrily entered her room.

GWAAAARRRRRRRR!

Rangda leaned down into her unmade bed and sniffed the blood and pus-covered pillow deeply.

SNIFF SNIFF SNIFF!

Suddenly she stopped sniffing, turned to Nabila, and pointed an accusing finger.

"I'm sorry, I was just really tired," said Nabila.

Rangda waved her finger back and forth as if to say, "no, no" and jumped over her bed toward Nabila.

Pietro turned back into a werewolf and blocked Rangda from Nabila.

Rangda's long, curved tusks opened wide, and a huge red tongue flopped over Pietro and licked Nabila.

"Guys, help!" she screeched. "Why did you leave me in here all alone?"

Pietro jumped up to bite Rangda's tongue, but before he could, she turned. Her eyes bugged out even farther than before, staring at all of us.

The monsters were ready to pounce. Twenty-Three and Grigore approached her, and Pietro was still behind her, making sure she didn't turn around and harm Nabila.

Rangda lifted her foot and brought it down on the ground. The room quaked. She lifted her hands high. The monsters readied for the attack.

"Waiiiiiiit!" I yelled. "Wait, Rangda! Tikoloshe has been lying to you. He's not really going to help."

She put her hands down for a moment and stared at me. She let out a low growl from between her tusks.

"Hear me out!" I said. "And I know it's going to be hard for you because you're his number one fan, but what I'm about to say is true. Tikoloshe is a trickster. He doesn't really want to help you guys! He's probably just using you."

She shook her head and turned to Nabila again. "Snackie!!!!"

Pietro jumped up to bite her arm, but she swatted him away.

She was HUNGRY.

Pietro hit the floor with an OOOOF and turned back into a human.

The other monsters were enraged.

"Everyone, please, wait!" I cried out in desperation. I looked at Director Z.

"STOP!" Director Z ordered.

Everyone stopped. Everyone but Rangda. Rangda moved forward.

"Rangda, please, just listen!" I said. "If I'm wrong, you can eat Nabila."

"What?!" yelled Nabila. "You can't just say that!"

"What has Tikoloshe done for you? You're all still old. You just think you're not old. But look in a mirror.

Take a minute and really think about it, and you'll know that things haven't gotten any better than before. In fact, things might just be worse."

Rangda pulled her tongue back into her mouth and tapped her tusk thoughtfully.

"That's right," I said. "Just think about it."

Ben motioned for Nabila to crawl out of the bed and come to us. She slowly, quietly started to move.

"You were probably fine in Bali, right?" I asked Rangda, trying to keep her attention. "And then you had a sudden urge to come here, and when you got here, you felt young. But Tikoloshe has made all of you just *think* you're young. He's tricked you. Even François is still old, but Tikoloshe has somehow charmed him so his fur looks young."

"Maybe you're the one tricking me," she said. She turned to see Nabila creeping away and ROARED.

Grigore, Gil, Clive, and Twenty-Three pounced forward to protect Nabila, but Rangda was going full speed.

ROOOOOOOOAAAAAR!

She pushed through all of them and opened her bright red mouth. Her mouth was open so wide that her tusks quivered.

"WAIT!" someone bellowed from the door. "Listen to me. You must stop!"

Rangda turned to look at François.

"Even though I've been stripped of my pendant," he said, "you know you must listen to me."

Rangda let out one last growl in anger. She knew she had to obey her Director.

"Now say you're sorry," François said.

Rangda turned to Nabila and said, "I'm sorry, snackie."

"Apology accepted," Nabila said. She put out her hand to shake Rangda's hand, but Rangda extended her tongue instead. Nabila shook it. "That's the last you'll taste of me," Nabila said.

"And now it's my turn to apologize," said François. "I'm sorry. I made a huge mistake."

Director
in Distress

"Had things really gotten so bad here that you had to call Tikoloshe?" I asked François.

"When the moon—the First Monster—shook and screamed and was drained of its energies," said François, "I panicked, I admit. We're so isolated here that I didn't have any colleagues to check in with about what was really happening. I thought it was the end."

"Yes, I had never heard of this facility before," said Director Z.

"We're a very private community," said François.

"Is that why you're on Twitter?" asked Shane.

François ignored Shane and continued. "So with

nobody to turn to, I panicked and called on the power of the demon imp Tikoloshe, thinking that his dark energy could help us in our time of need. I thought he would replenish our batteries, so to speak. I went to a local witch doctor and he made the statue that you bowed down to. That's the same statue we used, the witch doctor and I, to call him here."

François hung his head in shame.

"As soon as he got here," he continued, "he took my pendant and stripped me of my powers. Even as the moon regained its strength, our residents got weaker, but he gave them the illusion of strength."

"So that's why I got called here," I said. "And now I can't leave because I have yet to fulfill my duty—to save this place from Tikoloshe and make you the Director again."

"He told me to make a shrine using his statue, to make everyone bow down and pledge their allegiance. To keep his statue safe and clean at all times. I've bowed down to him like everyone else," continued François. "I've promised to do what he told me, and I've believed the lies he told me and the rest of the residents about how he would make us stronger. I lied, too. I lied to my own residents."

He flapped his leathery wings and shook his body wildly. His fur went from brown to gray. "Tikoloshe thought it would help me maintain control if I looked younger than the residents. Even I thought I was young again. Then your friend pushed me, and I was reminded. Oh, how I was reminded."

François put a wing over his face and cried.

"Thank you, François," I said, walking over to comfort him. "But why are we even talking about this? Tikoloshe can be invisible, right? Couldn't he be nearby?"

"He can when he wants to be," said François, wiping his tears away. "But I assure you, I can always tell when Tikoloshe is nearby, and he's not here now. But when he does come, we're going to be done for."

François started to cry again. The other monsters that had wandered in during his long confession hung their heads with him.

"No, you're not done for," said Director Z. "We're going to be just fine. You mustn't fear Tikoloshe. We know where his power lies: In that statue you made us bow to. In the same statue that you used to call him to you."

"I don't understand," said François. "My poor brain is so tired."

"Wait, I get it now!" I said, turning to Director Z. "I'm remembering back to when you saved the statue from the candle in the tower, François. You were terrified it would burn. Tikoloshe told you to treat the statue with respect, to protect it, but he didn't tell you why. He didn't want anyone to know."

"Know what?" asked Director Z.

"That the statue is his source of power," I said. "If we destroy it, he'll lose his grip on The House of Eternal Rest. Why else would he care about the statue? It would be meaningless to him."

"Well, let's hurry up and destroy the thing," said Gordon.

"Yes, now more than ever, we need to move quickly," said Director Z. "While we were searching for clues, I spoke with Principal Prouty. Things are not going well at home—"

"My grades?!" asked Ben. He turned white. "Are my grades okay? Have the Nurses ruined them?"

"Everything is as it was, and the Nurses are doing the best they can to impersonate you in your home and at school. But your parents are now well aware that something is wrong, and we can't continue the charade much longer."

"What happened?" I asked.

"It was a combination of us doing this for far too long—it's been a month now, you know—and the fact that your father just came back from Afghanistan," said Director Z.

"Dad's home?" I asked, suddenly feeling homesick.

"It took a lot of doing, but we were able to have someone meet him at the airport," continued Director

Z. "I feel bad for him, having served our country so well, only to be tricked when he got home. Still, as well as we did covering up your disappearance, your father's return upset the whole balance, and I fear we have only a few more days to keep the illusion in place."

"We'd better get back, then," said Nabila.

"All right," said François. "To the tower! Rangda, tweet to all your followers about what's happening. And I suggest you change your handle."

"Let's get the statue," said Gordon, running out of Rangda's room. "Yeah. YeaaaAAAAAAHHHH, NO!"

Gordon clutched his face and fell to the ground.

Lakes of Snakes

Gordon moaned in pain.

The monsters stopped in their tracks.

"What is it?" I said, rushing over to him.

"My zit!" moaned Gordon. "The big one. It hurts so bad again. Like it's drilling into my head."

I looked at his face and saw the swollen, ugly, massive red bubble on his forehead. It jiggled a little.

"Oh man, is something moving in there?" asked Ben. He choked back a little barf. "HHHHHWhat should we do?"

"Don't make fun of me," Gordon said to Ben. "Your zits aren't looking so good, either."

Ben felt the bumps all over his face and looked panicked.

There *was* something moving inside Gordon's zit, but I couldn't let him know. "It probably just got annoyed when the soccer ball hit your face," I said as calmly as I could.

"I need a mirror," said Gordon. "Who's got a mirror? I've got to pop this thing."

I looked over at Shane and Nabila, shook my head, and mouthed, *I don't think he should pop it.*

"There's one in my room, dearie," said Betty.

"All right, we can't let Gordon do this alone," I said. "Monsters, get up to that statue and destroy it!"

"You heard what he said," said François. "Move it."

My friends and I rushed down to Betty's room. There was a small bathroom with a toilet and a sink.

Gordon looked into the mirror at the massive, swollen zit on his face. He raised his index fingers toward his forehead . . .

"Get ready," I said to the others.

"Ready?" Gordon asked. "What do you guys have to get ready for?"

I looked around the bathroom for something to defend myself from the snake when it flew out of Gordon's face. I saw an oversize toilet plunger.

"I really don't think you should pop that," said Shane.

"I can't take it anymore," moaned Gordon. "It's got to go!"

"I wish I had the courage," said Ben, peering into the mirror. "But I'm just going to have to let these pop on their own."

"Did your zits just double in size?" I asked Ben.

"I don't know," he shrieked. "This is the first time I've seen them."

Gordon positioned his fingers on either side of the zit and grunted hard. The zit turned an ugly white but stayed intact.

Gordon brought his hands down. "Arrrrgh, this is so frustrating!"

"It's okay," said Shane. "You should leave it alone. That was—"

But before Shane could finish his sentence, Gordon planted his thumbs on either side of the zit, gritted his teeth, and bore down on the zit double-time.

"GRRRRRRRR," Gordon grunted, and sweat began to pour down his face.

He paused for a moment, took a deep breath, and then pushed his thumbs into either side again.

"AHHHHHHHHHH!" Gordon screamed, shaking as he pressed harder and harder until—

CRUNCHSPLAT!

A huge snake, along with a spray of blood and pus, flew out of Gordon's forehead, hit the mirror with a

FWAP, and plopped into the sink.

Gordon was so relieved, he had no idea what had happened. "YEAH!" he yelled. "That felt GREAT!"

Ben, who was so white now that his zits looked beet-red, moved to the side so Gordon could reach the toilet paper.

I raised the plunger like a baseball bat and approached the sink.

HISSSSSSSS!

The snake shot out of the sink straight at my face.

"Aaaargh!" I yelled, hitting the snake with the plunger before it could sink its tiny little dagger teeth into my face. It flopped onto the floor and slithered toward the door.

"Get out of here!" Nabila yelled. She jumped up as the snake quickly slithered between her feet and out of Betty's room.

"Guys!" yelled Ben. "When the snake hissed, something happened to my face."

"What do you mean?" asked Shane.

"Ben!" Nabila screeched, pointing.

The zits on his face had grown almost Gordon-size.

I reached up to feel my face boiling over, too.

"Yeah, I think you should pop those," said Shane. "Just aim in that direction." Shane pointed to the door.

GURRRRRPLE GWUUURBLE GLUB!

The toilet started to bubble, and a huge snake with

red eyes slithered out and flopped onto the floor.

HISSSSSSSSS.

"Everyone out!" I yelled.

As I turned to run, I could hear the toilet bubble again.

FLOP.

"Another one!" Shane yelled.

Tiny snakes poured out of the vents in the hallway. We had to dodge them as we ran down the hall and passed the cave room with the hole in the ceiling.

FLOP HISS FLOP HISS FLOP HISS.

Snakes were pouring in and made a scaly, slithering lake in the center of the room.

"They're coming from everywhere!" Nabila yelled.

We sprinted down the hall, and at the exact moment we couldn't hear the hissing anymore, Ben fell to his knees and clutched his face.

"My face!" he yelled. "It feels all hot and bubbly. Ugh, now I know how that zombie corpse that fell on me felt."

"Let me see," I said.

He moved his hands and—

POP! POP! POP!

Three snakes flew out of Ben's zits and hit my chest.

"Eeee!" I yelled, and brushed off the snake.

STOMP!

Roy crushed the snakes with his massive furry foot.

"Roy!" I yelled. "Help us!"

"Help you?" he said. "Help me! There are snakes everywhere!" He ran past us and kept going in the direction we had come from.

"Wait!" I yelled. "There are more that way!"

Roy turned around. "Then we're trapped!" he said. "They're upstairs, too!"

"Guys?" whimpered Ben. "I think one is still in my face."

"Oh man, he's got a tail coming out of that other zit," Gordon said.

"Well, don't just stand there," yelled Ben. "Get it out!"

Shane leaned down and snatched the tail. He pulled the snake out slowly.

"Arrgh!" said Ben. "It feels so gross!"

"Almost," said Shane.

SCHLOOOCK!

The snake came out, and Shane tossed it.

It hit Roy.

EEEEEEEEE!

"What were you thinking?" yelled Roy.

"Sorry," said Shane.

HISSSSSSSSSS.

"The snakes are getting closer," I said. "Everybody, let's move."

We ran down the hallway and toward the main

section of the dungeon. Just when we hit the main room, a river of snakes of all shapes and sizes slithered down the stairs. Each one had eyes that glowed red.

"I told you the snakes were this way," said Roy.

HISSSSSSSSSSS.

The snakes from the hallway slithered in.

We were surrounded.

"What are we going to do?" Nabila asked.

I held up my pendant. "Snakes, obey your master!"

The snakes slithered even closer.

"Not quite yet, my friends!" yelled a high-pitched voice. I felt like it was right next to me.

Something snatched my pendant out of my hand and floated in the air in front of me.

"These children deserve to die, yes they do," said the voice. Slowly, Tikoloshe's leathery, wart-covered face appeared, crooked nose first, in front of me. "But not yet."

He was barely three and a half feet tall. He looked like a mess, from his crazy hair to his holey clothes to his dirty feet that scratched impatiently at the floor. He stared at the pendant with bug eyes.

"Man, you're even uglier in person," said Gordon.

Tikoloshe threw back his head and giggled an insane giggle.

Immediately, another huge zit formed on Gordon's forehead.

Enter Tikoloshe

Tikoloshe's snakes herded us into the main room of the dungeon and then surrounded us. François and I stood in the center, away from everyone else.

"I take it that you didn't destroy the statue?" I asked François.

"Do you even need to bring it up?" he asked.

"Where's Director Z?" I asked.

A giant serpent, the biggest of Tikoloshe's snakes I had seen so far, slithered into the room with Director Z in its jaws. It put him down gently next to me and then slithered away.

"Serpent fangs are one of the few things in this

world that can ruin my suits," said Director Z. "I knew I should have packed a spare."

I looked around to see that all of my friends and all of the monsters from Gallow Manor were still here. There were fewer residents of The House of Eternal Rest, and many of the ones that remained were barely able to stand.

I looked up at the monkey on my shoulder. "How have you been? I almost forgot you were there." He gave me a small thumbs-up with his little black monkey hand.

"What happened?" I asked François.

"There was much confusion," said François. "The few residents who were with us in the room to hear my confession knew what was happening. Many others did not, and we were slowed down on the way to the tower. The adzes were especially upset, and it didn't help that while I tried to explain to them what was going on, as we neared the entrance to the tower, Tikoloshe and his snakes began their relentless attack."

François's eyes began to well with tears.

"The residents who didn't know what was happening with Tikoloshe—that he was the enemy—didn't put up any fight at all. They were eaten alive."

"Why haven't we been eaten alive?" I asked.

"I think we're about to find out," said Director Z, and he pointed ahead.

Tikoloshe walked into the room with the three

adzes buzzing excitedly around his head. He walked toward Director Z, François, and me. The snakes that were in front of us parted as he made his way.

"Well, well, well," said Tikoloshe in his high voice. "I thought The House of Eternal Rest was all mine. Until you two came along." He wiggled a gnarled, dirty finger at Director Z and me.

"François," Tikoloshe said, turning to face him. "Ooooooh, I'm quite disappointed in you."

François was at least twice the size of Tikoloshe, but the large bat shook with fear. The small imp reached up and slapped François's cheek a few times.

SLAP SLAP SLAP.

"Bad bat," Tikoloshe scolded. "Very bad bat." SLAP "I hope that the pain . . ." SLAP ". . . I unleashed upon your residents . . ." SLAP ". . . with my slithery friends . . ." SLAP SLAP ". . . will keep you from making such a stupid mistake in the future."

"You are too kind, Master," whimpered François. "I am here to serve you."

"Oh, you'll serve me, for sure," said Tikoloshe. "But you're not second-in-command anymore! Kossi, the lead adze, will now keep an eye on you while I'm away. Grace and Hervé, the other adzes, will assist him. I have many places to be. I'm quite busy all over Africa, but I'll soon gather my forces here. Yes, once things are in order elsewhere."

Tikoloshe rubbed one of the two pendants—my pendant—between his fingers and giggled.

"Oooh, I'm glad you showed up, young American," Tikoloshe said to me. He walked right up to me, lifted the pendant, stuck out a slimy black tongue, and licked it. "The more power, the merrier," he said around his tongue.

"Why do you need this power?" I said. "Leave these old monsters alone."

"Oh, I don't *need* this power," Tikoloshe said. "I didn't even *want* this power. But now that I'm here, there's no stopping me."

"Monsterdom is recovering from its worst setback in history," Director Z said, stepping up. "Only by working together shall—"

Tikoloshe held up a hand. "Oh, blah, blah, blah, boohoo, human," he said. "I *know* monsterdom is recovering from its worst setback in history. The timing is perfect. Everyone is so weak!"

"But if you don't need this power," I said, "why bother?"

"Because it's just so much fun," said Tikoloshe, doing a little dance as he slipped my pendant over his head. "My life has been getting pretty stressful. Work is hard. Why, just before I got here, I was in South Africa pestering a family, pretending to be the spirit of their dead grandfather, setting them against one another

153

while his will was figured out. That's some hard work! When I was called through my statue to this place, I saw a great opportunity—a chance to build my powers, up, up, up! Not just here in Africa, but everywhere in the world. And the best part was—it would be easy!

"The minds of monsters all over the world are so weak. I willed monsters here from thousands of miles away. I whispered sweet nothings in their ears, made them crazy with false hope. I made them think they were younger than they were, all the while sapping their energies and building up my powers."

"Fine," I said. "I give up. I pledged my allegiance to you. I'll cooperate in any way you like. But leave the monsters alone."

"Chris!" gasped Director Z.

"Oh, those silly words that François made you say?" said Tikoloshe. "Those were meaningless. I was just playing with you. I don't need your allegiance or your life. But when the time is right and your energies are ripe, I will kill you and steal the energies of your afterlife. Oh, it was a HOOT watching you all bow down. And that trick François pulled on Roy? So worth having my statue almost break. Ah-ha-ha-ha-ha!"

"You were there for that?" I asked.

"Oh, yeah, he was there for that," said François. "He was the one who gave me the idea."

"You. Never. Know. When. I'll. Be. There," said Tikoloshe.

I got so angry that my face itched and crawled. "You're nothing but a bully," I screamed, and as I screamed . . .

POP!

. . . my head shot back.

A small snake flew at Tikoloshe as I fell into Director Z's arms.

Tikoloshe dodged the snake quickly, and it hit the floor with a plop.

"Go find your friends, little one," said Tikoloshe.

The snake slithered away, leaving a trail of pus behind it.

My face throbbed.

"Oh, I see you've been enjoying the gift I gave you," giggled Tikoloshe. "That's going to get worse before it gets better. Yes, much worse, if you disobey me! If the snake zits aren't enough to convince you to behave, this lovely creature will ensure that you do."

POP!

With a flash, Kossi, the lead adze, took human form and walked directly toward me.

He looked deep into my eyes.

I want you to be very, very frightened, said Kossi's voice in my head.

"I am frightened," I said back.

"What are you doing?" Director Z asked. "Kossi, look away this instant!"

"How does it look inside the young American's mind?" Tikoloshe asked. "Is it empty? Tell me it's empty."

"Empty, my lord," Kossi hissed as he looked through my eyes and into my brain. "Very empty, indeed."

Tikoloshe giggled.

Now, keep looking frightened. This will not take long. I am sorry. But look terrified for me.

I began to cry.

"Leave me alone," I whimpered.

"Chris!" Director Z yelled. He grabbed me by the shoulders, but a huge boa constrictor wrapped itself around his leg and yanked him back.

Listen very closely to me. I am tricking the trickster. I promised Tikoloshe my services. But I side with you. I side with us. Tikoloshe has one weakness. I cannot speak of it, for fear of being heard, even after Tikoloshe leaves us. But I can tell you with my mind. Inkanyamba, the Master Serpent of Africa, is not under Tikoloshe's control. Until Tikoloshe controls Inkanyamba, he won't truly have control of the snakes and slitheries of Africa, as Inkanyamba could take them back at any time. Do you understand?

"Please leave me alone," I said. Tears fell down my cheeks. I had to make sure Tikoloshe had no clue what Kossi was telling me.

Yes, I thought back at Kossi. *Where is Inkanyamba?*

Grace knows, said Kossi. *When the time is right, she will tell you. For now, you must head to the first facility, the place we used to live.*

Kossi let go of my mind, and I fell to the ground. Director Z was still there, trapped by the boa constrictor.

"Chris?" he asked. "Are you okay?"

I winked at Director Z.

"Are we good?" asked Tikoloshe.

"Yes, my lord," growled Kossi.

"Now, everybody behave," said Tikoloshe, "or the plague that I'm putting the children through will get even worse! Kossi and the snakes will guard you. I'm off to plan my glorious plans!"

Crossing Snake Plain

Soon after Tikoloshe left, the snakes slithered out of the large main room.

"Something tells me they haven't gone far," said Shane, walking over to me. "Are you okay?"

Grigore stormed over to Kossi, his fangs bared.

"How dare you violate my friend like that?" yelled Grigore.

"Wait!" I yelled. "Grigore, stop!"

"Bring it on!" yelled Kossi.

"No, Kossi, we can't keep up this act," I said. "There's no time for it."

"What are you talking about?" Director Z asked.

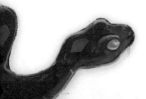

"I can't say," I said. "It's too dangerous, and we don't have enough time to go into detail. You just have to trust me."

The monsters grumbled and shuffled, unsure about what was happening.

Grace flew up to my ear. The monkey covered my earhole protectively.

EEEEEEEEEEEEK!

"No, it's fine," buzzed Grace quietly. "I will not hurt him. You can trust me."

The monkey released its grip on my ear. Grace landed in my earhole so only I could hear what she said.

"Inkanyamba hides under rocks in the bend of the river directly between the ruin and the retirement home," she buzzed. "But only the robot can retrieve her."

I thought for a moment and remembered the robot next to the busted tank in the abandoned retirement center.

"Of course!" I said. "It all makes sense now." I remembered the fang we had seen in the hole in the wall of the retirement facility, and the tank. It must have been Inkanyamba! She must have broken off a few teeth while escaping to the river. "But why do we even need her now? Let's just finish the job we started."

I ran to the back of the ruin, and everyone else followed.

The entrance to the tower was surrounded by

snakes. The door was open, and the staircase was chockablock full of them!

"So that's where they all went," Shane said.

My face started to bubble.

"Back away!" I yelled. "We can't let the snakes see us! We're supposed to be behaving, remember?"

I ran out to the next room and looked out of a window. A large, winged serpent flew around the tower.

"What does this all mean?" asked Director Z, desperate to know.

The others looked around, confused.

"What's going on?" asked Rangda.

"The monsters of Gallow Manor and I are going to the abandoned retirement home," I replied. "Anyone strong enough can come with, but we're leaving now."

I ran back to the entryway and tromped down the stairs without thinking.

"All right," I said. "Let's do this."

Bright lights flashed in front of my eyes, and my head was in a vise once again.

"ARG," I moaned. "I forgot." I tried to turn around, but passed out on the bottom stair.

Shane rushed down and grabbed me.

"Stupid rule," I mumbled.

"Are you okay?" asked Shane.

"Just give me a minute," I said as he helped me up the stairs. "I just need my brain to cool off."

"What if you bring everyone along?" asked Shane. "If all the monsters come, then you won't be abandoning them and your headaches are cured!"

A few minutes later, everyone—my friends and the monsters of The House of Eternal Rest—stood at the edge of the completely silent field. The abandoned retirement home stood on the other side.

"This is too good to be true," said Shane. "Which means it's probably not true."

FLASH! BOOOOOOOOOOM!

Lightning struck the field in front of us, and the skies darkened. The clouds opened up, and a heavy rain began to fall.

"Told ya," Shane said.

"I think the rain will be the least of our problems," I said.

The sound of pouring rain was shattered by the screeches of meerkats. The small, furry creatures started climbing out of holes in the ground.

"They're coming from everywhere!" yelled Shane.

The creatures jumped out of every hole and rushed for the river. They ran through the grassy field and swam across as fast as they could. They scurried up onto the shore on the other side and kept running.

"Something must have really scared them," said Ben.

"I'll give you one guess," I said.

Before Ben could guess, red-eyed snakes slithered out of every meerkat hole in the field. Small snakes came out twenty at a time, bunched together in tight clumps. Huge boas burst through the holes and practically shot up into the air.

François looked up into the trees behind us and yelled, "Get ready."

The huge fruit bats woke up and shook the water off their wings.

"Thank goodness everyone ended up coming," Shane said. "We need everyone's help to cross Snake Plain."

Director Z turned to me. "You've got this," he said.

"Run!" I yelled.

We rushed forward in the pouring rain.

"It's so hard to see!" yelled Nabila.

"Just look out for the glowing red eyes," said Shane.

"Stronger monsters, move ahead," I yelled. "Weaker monsters, stay behind, but not too far behind. I don't want to get a headache."

Grigore, Rangda, Roy, and Pietro took the lead.

CRACK BOOM!

Lightning struck the trees around the plain.

"And try not to get electrocuted!" I yelled.

Hundreds of snakes closed in, but they were quickly pushed back.

Pietro was biting snakes just behind their head and

flinging them away. His wet muzzle was red with blood.

Bats flew down and plucked up the smaller snakes, or flapped their wings in front of the larger ones when they got too close to monsters.

"Nooooo!" yelled a zombie behind us as a large snake wrapped around its body and squeezed.

Shane turned back to help, stunning the snake with a karate chop.

Other zombies weren't so lucky.

A cobra reared up in front of Hervé and struck. With a POP, the adze turned back into a firefly before the cobra could sink its teeth into him.

I dodged the holes in the ground I could see. The monkey, soaking wet, its fur slicked against its body, screeched when I almost stepped into the ones I missed. But it was hard to see through the rain. Before I knew what was happening, a huge cobra popped out of a hole directly in front of me.

SCREEEEEEEE!

The monkey squealed, but there was nothing I could do.

The cobra reared up its head to strike . . .

. . . and was pulled back into the ground.

"What?" I said, amazed.

A few holes over, Twenty-Three scurried out, dragging the cobra by its tail.

Pietro came over and finished it off.

"We're halfway there!" I yelled. "Everyone keep moving!"

I looked back and saw more snakes and chaos. Some monsters fell. Others kept going.

Gordon ran up to my side, and even in the pouring rain, I could see that his zits had gotten terrible. Little red eyes glowed through a dozen raised spots on his skin.

"Gordon," I yelled as he ran past, "you've got to do something about those zits!"

"As soon as we get there," said Gordon. He ran even faster—it was practically clear in front of us.

"Hurry!" I yelled.

All of a sudden Gordon disappeared.

"What?!" I screeched. "Gordon, where are you?!"

I ran up to the edge of a huge hole filled with mud and massive snakes.

"Chris, help!" Gordon screeched, desperately trying to claw his way out. "It's a python pit!"

One snake snagged him and pulled him into the pile.

Another wrapped itself around him and bit him on the face. He stopped moving.

"NOOOOO!" I yelled.

Fighting Snakes
with Snakes

I looked around for someone who could help.

"ROY," I yelled, "get over here now!"

Roy ran over, and I pointed to the python pit.

Without a word, Roy jumped in and began punching the python that had a grip on Gordon. He kicked the others that tried to get close. His fur was so slippery in the rain, the snakes couldn't get a hold of him.

Roy finally pulled Gordon out. His face bled terribly.

I ran over to help Gordon while Roy swatted other snakes away.

"Gordon!" I slapped his face. "Gordon!"

The rain washed away the blood.

Gordon's face didn't have a scratch.

"Gordon!" I yelled.

My friend opened his eyes.

"That python bit my zits," Gordon said. "Two fangs in two zits."

"Now you have no more zits!" I said.

"Awesome!" he yelled, and jumped up. "YEAH!"

Shane ran up to us. His face was a wreck.

I looked ahead to see Ben and Nabila with most of the monsters, waving us into the abandoned retirement home.

"Let's go!" I said. "We're so close."

"I think I've got to pop these right now," said Shane. "They hurt so much, and the snakes are just going to keep growing." He dropped to his knees, and I could see his face. It didn't look pretty.

Snakes were closing in, but we had to do something.

"Grab a snake and let it bite your zit," I said to Shane.

"What?" asked Shane.

"Trust me," I said.

"Just be careful," said Gordon. "I think it only works if you get the fang to go right into the zit! Otherwise . . ."

We knew what would happen otherwise.

We dodged a massive boa constrictor, then Roy quickly bonked it on the head and used it like a huge whip to clear a space for us.

"Shane, hurry!" I yelled. "Your face is squirming!"

Shane grabbed a smaller snake by the tail. "This is crazy," said Shane. The snake struggled in his hand, striking the air as Shane held it back.

Gordon ran over and grabbed the head as soon as it struck again. Its open mouth hissed into the air.

"Oh man, I can feel them moving," said Shane.

"Hold tight!" yelled Gordon. He brought the serpent's fangs closer to Shane's face and carefully dug a fang deep into one of Shane's zits.

"It hurts so much," said Shane, falling backward.

Shane was facedown and twitching on the field.

"Shane!" I yelled. "Shane!"

He rolled over, and I could see the snakes under his skin turning black and dying.

"Yeah, I forgot to tell you how much it hurt," Gordon said.

CRACK! BOOM!

Lightning struck the python pit, sending smoking snakes into the air.

"We've got to get off the plain," I said. "Shane, can you run?"

"Let's do it!" Shane said, jumping up.

Roy, Shane, Gordon, and I ran for it, jumping over snakes before they could bite us.

Once we made it inside, François and Rangda took care of the few snakes that had followed us in, and then there were no more.

"Where'd they go?" asked Shane.

"To take a nap?" I wondered. "I wish I could take a nap."

I took a moment to catch my breath and watched the rain stop. The monkey got off of my shoulder and lay down at my feet.

The sun came out, and all of the monsters and kids smelled like the biggest wet dog after rolling around in the biggest cat turd.

"So what are we doing here, Boss?" Director Z asked me.

I pointed at the robot next to the tank.

"Care to elaborate?" asked Director Z.

Nabila moaned and clutched her face.

"Oh man, they feel terrible," said Nabila. "So weird."

"Hurry," I said. "Find a snake. If we can get one to bite your zit, then you'll be cured."

"Out on the plain?" Shane asked. He rushed out of the hole in the wall. "Where did they all go? I don't like that we don't know where they all went."

"Maybe my fang vill vork?" asked Grigore.

"Oh, good idea, brother," Kossi said.

POP.

"Too late," said Pietro.

I turned to Nabila. One snake had burst out of her face. She held on to it tightly—not an easy task with all of the pus.

"I don't believe it," I said.

Her other zits quivered and shook, ready to pop, but before they could . . .

"Eat this," Nabila said, and moved the snake's mouth over to her biggest zit.

HISSSSSBITE.

It took a huge bite. Nabila tossed the snake over to Ben. "Catch," she said.

Ben caught it with a squeal and latched it onto his zit.

They both fell to the floor, writhing in pain.

"Don't worry," said Gordon. "The pain disappears pretty quickly."

I walked over to the robot and looked it up and down.

"I've got to figure out how it works," I said to myself. "I don't even know what to do with it when I do. But how are we going to make it back to the other building?"

"We're going back?!" yelled Gordon.

"Shhhhh!" I said. "Keep it down. Yes, we are going back."

My friends and the monsters crowded around.

"There's no time to explain, but we've got to go back now," I whispered, "and we've got to bring the robot with us. I wish we had more help. We barely made it across the first time." I turned to François. "Raven Hill Retirement Home had SWAT gear for the Nurses. Does this facility have any armor or arms?"

"Hey, where are your Nurses, anyway?" asked Ben.

"It's funny you ask—" François started. But the monkey interrupted with a screech.

EEEEEEEEEEEEE!

François gave the monkey a funny look and said, "Unfortunately, no. We don't have anything defensive or offensive."

"Defensive or offensive," mumbled Gordon. "Hey, that gives me an idea. Remember how hard I was bashed in the face with that soccer ball?"

"What?" I said. "We can't ask the soccer kids for help. Even if they believe us, what if they get hurt?"

"They'll be so far away, they won't be near any danger," said Gordon. "Remember how far I was when I was knocked down?"

"That sounds so crazy, it just might work," said Shane.

"I know they have the power," said Gordon. "Now I need to see if they can focus that power and aim."

"What makes you think that they'll help us out?" asked Ben.

"I've got an idea," said Gordon. He ran out of the hole in the wall and around the corner of the building.

"Gordon, wait!" I yelled, but he was already gone. I turned to the others. "All right, let's figure out how this robot works."

I stepped up to the massive, twenty-foot robot to see if I could find a way in.

"What's this button do?" I wondered out loud. But before I could press it . . .

EEEEEEEEEEEEEK!

The monkey jumped up onto the robot and swatted my hand away.

"What is it with you and this robot?" I asked the monkey.

It screeched again and crawled farther up the robot.

"Get offa there!" I yelled, and I pulled the monkey down. "Shane, come over here and help me. Director Z, have you ever seen anything like this?"

EEEEEEEEEEEEEK!

Roy held me up so I could look at the robot's head. The monkey was getting angrier.

EEEEEEEEEEEEEK!

There was a small door in the back that I could see through the eyes in the front, but I couldn't open it. Ben tried, Nabila tried. We all failed.

EEEEEEEEEEEEEK!

"Um, Chris," Nabila said, stepping down from Roy's shoulder.

She pointed at the door into the laboratory.

A very angry Tikoloshe stood in the doorway. Behind him were more snakes and serpents than we had seen all day long. They were ready to attack.

Oh, It's on Now!

"I leave you for an hour, and this is what happens?" he yelled. "Kossi, you have a lot of explaining to do."

"Bite me," hissed Kossi.

"Well, that explains everything, then," said Tikoloshe.

I high-fived Kossi, while looking away from his eyes.

"My slitheries, loyal as they are, let me know that something was going on," said Tikoloshe. "I will reward them by feeding you to them. I've had enough! I—"

There was a huge CLANK, and an electric whirring sound filled the room.

The robot moved its arm.

"What the—" I said. I looked up and could see the monkey working some sort of controls behind the eyes of the robot.

"I always wondered how that worked," Rangda said.

"Just *what* do you think you're going to do with that robot?" Tikoloshe yelled. "And did I hear you say you were headed back to the ruin? Yes, I did, but why on earth would you want to go back? Everyone is here! Everything is here! Everything but . . ."

A lightbulb went on in Tikoloshe's head.

"My statue!" he screeched. "No!"

He lifted up a gnarled hand and waved it at me. My face exploded in pain as dozens of zits bubbled up.

Tikoloshe ran past us and out. "Noooooooooo!"

"Goooooo!" I yelled. I could barely talk because of the zits around my mouth, but I couldn't slow everyone down. "We have to get the statue before he does. If he hides it, he'll have power over The House of Eternal Rest forever."

The snakes slithered quickly into the room as we ran out onto the plain once again. The robot was slow but picking up speed.

Once everyone was out of the room, the three adzes stood at the hole in the wall and stared down the snakes. Their bodies trembled as they tried to control the hundreds of writhing, angry, hungry reptiles.

Up ahead, Tikoloshe fell into the python pit.

"Yeah!" yelled Gordon.

With an angry grunt, Tikoloshe pulled himself out of the hole.

"No!" yelled Gordon.

Behind us, the adzes finally lost control, and the snakes slithered toward us.

"They're so fast," said Ben. "We're not going to make it to the other side!"

In the middle of the plain, the snakes caught up to us, some from behind and some from right below us, popping up through the meerkat holes.

Tikoloshe stopped near the ruin and sent more snakes our way.

The monsters struggled to keep the snakes under control.

"He's directing them!" I yelled. "Everyone, watch out! It's not going to be as easy here." A python reared up in front of me. The Monkey Robot kicked it in the face with a CRUNCH.

There were so many snakes that we were walking on a writhing carpet, just making sure that they didn't bite our feet. I was desperate for one of them to bite my face, but they were out of control—I couldn't risk getting bit in the wrong place.

I had to get the Monkey Robot to the river.

"Help that zombie!" I yelled, and the Monkey Robot

swung an arm, pushing a zombie away before a snake could strike its face.

I reached up to my face and it felt like it was melting off, but I knew I couldn't stop. I was the one who had to convince Inkanyamba to help.

"The robot and I need cover!" I screeched.

A serpent leaped directly for my arm, and the Monkey Robot slammed it hard. But even the monkey was fumbling to get all of the snakes off of the robot. Monkey Robot was slowing down.

"Over here!" yelled Gordon. He ran along the riverbank with a dozen kids from the soccer field.

"Ready," Gordon yelled.

The kids each dropped a soccer ball.

"Aim," Gordon yelled.

They pulled their legs back.

"FIIIIIIRE!"

A dozen soccer balls flew into the snakes, knocking them back with hard THUMPS.

"FIIIIIIIIRE!" Gordon yelled again.

More balls flew, and it was just enough distraction to allow the Monkey Robot and me to escape to the river.

"Yeah!" I yelled to Gordon. "Now get them out of here!"

As the kids ran back toward the town, I could see a new pair of shoes on Diblo's feet. They were Gordon's fancy state-of-the-art athletic shoes—his most prized possession. Diblo gave me a thumbs-up.

"So that's how he convinced them," I said.

I looked over my shoulder and saw the monsters and my friends slowly making their way to the ruin.

Now my face was on fire, but there wasn't a snake around to bite my zits. I just had to move forward.

Tikoloshe didn't seem to notice what Monkey Robot and I were doing. He was too worried about his statue. He turned to run to the tower and was bombarded by the fruit bats.

I hoped the bats and other monsters would hold him up long enough for me to gain control of the snakes and race to the tower.

I could feel the tiny snake babies moving in my face as the robot finally hit the water and walked into the deep center of the river. It bowed down and disappeared.

I looked over at the ruins and couldn't see Tikoloshe anymore.

"Hurry, Monkey Robot," I said to the water. "Hurry!"

With a great splash, the Monkey Robot rose from the water . . .

. . . with Inkanyamba in its arms.

My face hurt so bad, I swayed on my feet. But I had to keep going.

"Inkanyamba!" I yelled, raising my hands. "I might not have a pendant, but I have been sent by my pendant to help you. My pendant—and your retirement home—

were stolen by Tikoloshe, who has now taken control of your kingdom . . ."

I couldn't see over the bulges on my face, but I had to continue.

"You must take back the snakes. Follow me, and let's defeat this imp."

I put down my hands.

Inkanyamba bit down on something in her mouth and then spat it directly in my face.

My face exploded in pain, and I fell back onto the ground.

The Serpent Express

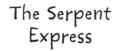

I was only out for a few seconds. When I woke up again, the pain in my face was gone, except for in one spot.

I reached up and felt something hard and thin stuck in my cheek.

I yanked it out—"YOW!"—and looked at it.

It was a fang from Inkanyamba.

I looked over to see that the battle had moved inside the ruin. I hoped there was still enough time.

I stood up quickly just as Monkey Robot set Inkanyamba down on the ground next to me.

"Thank you," I said.

Monkey Robot pointed at Inkanyamba's back.

"You want me to ride Inkanyamba?" I asked.

Monkey Robot nodded.

I jumped onto the giant wet serpent and held on to her back.

HISSSSSSSSSSSSSS.

The sound vibrated through the earth and through me. It made my toes tickle.

HISSSSSSSSSSSSSS.

There was silence from the ruin.

"Is she calling the snakes?" I asked Monkey Robot.

It nodded. Then it made a motion to "hold on."

I held on, and Inkanyamba shot forward, slithering quietly over the plain, past the bodies of dead snakes and destroyed monsters.

"Whoa!" I yelled as she glided up the stairs of the entrance and into the entryway.

Snakes were leaving the ruin. They stopped and bowed to their Master, and Inkanyamba hissed in return.

Inkanyamba sped to the room with the tower entrance. Snakes were pouring out into the jungle through the open wall of the ruins.

"He's up there!" yelled Director Z, watching me with amazement. "Hurry!"

Inkanyamba increased her speed and slithered up the spiral staircase.

We quickly crept up on Grigore and Kossi. "Watch

out!" I yelled. They turned into their flying forms and followed us.

As Inkanyamba burst through the doorway, I tumbled off to find Shane and Roy chasing Tikoloshe down.

"Stop!" I yelled.

Tikoloshe turned around and stuck out his tongue at me.

"You're too late," yelled Tikoloshe. "Oooh, I got slowed down when the snakes turned on me, but now I'm in control of the situation. I WIN."

He reached his shrine and screeched with excitement as he grabbed the statue.

"So pretty," he said, and kissed the statue. "Where shall I hide you?"

Inkanyamba hissed at the doorway.

"You have nowhere to go," I said.

"What, do you think this is the first time I've ever climbed down a tower?" giggled Tikoloshe.

"Get him," I yelled, and Inkanyamba shot forward.

Tikoloshe stuffed the statue in his pants and then turned invisible. Inkanyamba hit the back wall.

"Ha, it's safe now!" he yelled. "I can run around this place for all eternity and you'll never find me."

"Block the windows," I yelled.

Roy moved to a window and spread his arms.

Shane moved to another window. "Chris, look!" he

yelled. He pointed out of the window.

"Kongamato's coming!" I said. "Hit the floor!"

We all hit the cold floor just in time.

SCREEEEEEEEEE SMASH!

The tower shook, and the roof caved in halfway, sending a shower of bricks down on us.

"Ow!" I yelled. Bricks were hitting my legs, arms, and back.

SMACK.

A brick hit Tikoloshe right on the head, and he went from invisible to visible.

"Grab him!" I yelled.

Shane jumped forward and was just about to grab Tikoloshe when . . .

SCREEEEEEEEEE SMASH.

Kongamato hit the building again.

What was left of the roof was blown off with a powerful wing flap.

"That's enough," I yelled into the sky. "We've got this!"

But a very angry Kongamato returned and scooped up Tikoloshe.

The statue flew out of his hands, and Shane caught it.

"Help!" Tikoloshe screamed.

Kongamato flipped him in the air and caught him by the leg. Tikoloshe dangled upside down.

I saw both pendants fall from his neck.

I caught them and put them around my neck.

"Roy, would you like to do the honors?" asked Shane, holding up the statue.

"With pleasure," said Roy.

Shane slid the statue over to Roy, who stomped on it like it was a spider sandwich.

SMASH CRUNCH SMASH!

"Nooooooooooooo!" screamed Tikoloshe from the sky. "My beautiful statue."

Kongamato dropped Tikoloshe from above the tower.

"AHHHHHHHH!" yelled Tikoloshe as he fell.

Inkanyamba lifted up her head, opened her mouth, and . . .

GULP.

. . . ate Tikoloshe.

"Well done," I yelled.

"Yeah!" yelled Shane, and he high-fived Roy.

I patted Inkanyamba on the back.

BURP.

"I hope he doesn't give you indigestion," I said.

We all laughed. Even Inkanyamba.

The End

A few hours later, the ruins were quiet. Monsters lay around the stones, relaxing and chatting. My friends and I were talking with François and Director Z.

"Have you ever heard of a Ghanaian fantasy coffin?" Kossi asked Grigore as they passed by.

"No, but tell me more," said Grigore.

"Basically, they can create any coffin you can imagine," said Kossi. "It's just about the same size as a regular coffin, but in any shape you'd ever want. A car. A fish. A bat. A Coca-Cola can. A cow. Whatever."

"Oooh," said Grigore. "I'd have to think about vhat I vant. Anything?"

"Anything," said Kossi.

"It's so good to see everyone so happy," said François. "For as much as the battle wore them out, I think it brought some energy back into them as well."

"I'm sure it was good to see young monsters again," said Director Z. "Healthy monsters. Monsterdom might not be doomed, after all."

"Oh, speaking of bringing back the energy," I said, "I believe that this is your pendant."

I pulled François's pendant off of my neck and put it over his head.

"It feels good to be back," said François. "But are you sure you have to leave? You're more than welcome to stay and help out. You were a wonderful Director, and we'd hate to lose you."

"No," I said. "We've got to get back to the States. We've been away a long, long time."

"Don't worry, though," said Gordon. "I wouldn't be surprised if Diblo and the boys come knocking on your door and ask to help."

"Just make sure that claw thing is turned off," said Director Z, swallowing hard.

"Do you really have to leave right away?" asked François.

"We don't even have time for a nap on your tarantula bed," said Shane sadly.

"Would you like me to ship you one?" asked

François. "What's your address?"

"I don't think it would make it through customs," said Ben.

"So is Tikoloshe destroyed forever?" Nabila asked François.

"Tikoloshe is far too ancient to be destroyed," said François, "but traveling slowly down Inkanyamba's digestive tract will be good punishment. He'll come out later looking like a really angry piece of poop, but he'll certainly leave us alone."

"Better have a big pooper-scooper ready!" Nabila said.

We all laughed until the monkey that saved the day with the robot padded into the room. I squatted down and gave him a big hug.

"We couldn't have done it without you!" I said.

He chattered happily as a dozen other monkeys came into the room. He joined the other monkeys and went into the cafeteria, putting things in order for the move back to the abandoned facility. They cleaned up broken trays and placed utensils back where they belonged.

"It's good to have the Nurses back," said François.

"Wait, so that monkey was a Nurse?" asked Shane. "Huh, that's why he was always one step ahead of the game."

"Speaking of one step ahead of the game," I said,

"we'd better get going. What sort of monster transport is there around here?"

"Kongamato might be able to help you with some air-based transportation," said François.

"This has been an awesome journey," I said. "But I'm going to be happy to be back home!"

Epilogue

He Who Would Save Us saved us! His task complete, he journeyed safely to his home. Meanwhile, there was much work to be done at The House of Eternal Rest. I called my staff into the back of the cafeteria.

"Thank you for obeying me and staying far away from our poor old friends," I said. "Though I needed to keep an eye on the situation, it was best for you to take shelter in the jungle."

"It was hard," Dosufe said. "We're Nurses! But we knew it was right."

I patted him on his soft, hairy back.

"Thank you," I said. "Now that you are back, and

François is able to carry on, we can get down to the work of helping our dear residents get back to their normal lives or afterlives. Come now."

I walked through the cafeteria to the entryway beyond.

"Wait," said Lionel. "First, can you tell us everything that happened? We're dying to know."

"Yes, of course," I said, knowing it was an important story that would be passed down for generations. "Let me tell you about *He Who Would Save Us*."

My staff gathered closer.

"It was said that he would come. But when it happened, it wasn't a man in a huge silver plane, as I always thought it would be. No, it was a boy who rode on the backs of crocodiles . . ."

ABOUT THE AUTHOR . . .

M. D. Payne is a mad scientist who creates monsters by stitching together words instead of dead body parts. After nearly a decade in multimedia production for public radio, he entered children's publishing as a copywriter and marketer. Monster Juice is his debut series. He lives in the tiny village of New York City with his wife and baby girl, and hopes to add a hairy, four-legged monster to his family soon.